CU00924414

GOOSE OF HERMOGENES

GOOSE OF HERMOGENES

ITHELL
COLQUHOUN

PETER OWEN
London and Chester Springs

PETER OWEN PUBLISHERS
73 Kenway Road, London SW5 0RE

Peter Owen books are distributed in the USA by
Dufour Editions Inc., Chester Springs, PA 19425-0007

First published by Peter Owen Ltd 1961

ISBN 0 7206 1177 6

A catalogue record for this book is available from
the British Library

Printed and bound in Great Britain by
Bookmarque Ltd, Croydon, Surrey

*'It is our door-keeper, our balm, our
honey, oil, urine, maydew, mother, egg,
secret furnace, true fire, venomous dragon,
theriac, ardent wine, Green Lion, Bird of
Hermes, Goose of Hermogenes, two-edged
sword in the hand of the cherub that guards
the Tree of Life.'*

*Eirenaeus Philalethes:
Brevis Manductio ad Rubrem Coelestem*

Foreword by Peter Owen

I first met Ithell Colquhoun in the early 1950s, in a Soho pub called the Wheatsheaf, an establishment frequented by impecunious bohemians when they could afford to do so. Soho at that time was the haunt of writers, painters, down-and-outs, drunks, drug addicts and people on the fringes of the arts, some of whom subsequently became successful. I was there with the poet Thomas Blackburn and some others with an interest in writing. Ithell was of that party. At the time she was in her forties and still a very attractive woman: slim, with a soft and unaffected voice, ash-blonde hair and a fair complexion. She also had an endearing giggle. I was told that she was a painter and that she also wrote poetry. I bumped into her a number of times in the Wheatsheaf and I grew to like her. She was multi-talented, affable, with a vivid and unconventional imagination. Coming from a well-to-do family, she had a private income, and her background and education at Cheltenham Ladies' College gave her a veneer of respectability, but this was tempered by her exceptional creativity. She told me that she had written a short novel called *Goose of Hermogenes*, and I agreed to read it. The book was unusual and memorable, very well written, with a strong mystical element.

I had only just started publishing under my own imprint and had very little money, and I wasn't sure about whether I would be able to sell the novel. It was short, which at that time was problematic, as bookshops did not like books of only a hundred pages or so. I told her I would think about it, which I did, and from time to time she used to press me for an answer.

I got to know Ithell better after my marriage in 1953, as she became friends with my wife Wendy, and she often visited us in Holland Road, near Shepherd's Bush, for coffee. She once invited us to a dinner given by the PEN Club at the Rembrandt Hotel in South Kensington. It was there that I first met Peter Vansittart, whom I later published. Ithell and I continued to meet periodically at parties – in the 1950s and 1960s the less well off among our friends, many of them writers and artists, were famous for hosting so-called 'bottle parties', at which each guest contributed a bottle (a favourite was strong, cheap Merrydown cider), and Ithell often accompanied us or came over to our flat. Sometimes Wendy and I visited her studio in Windmill Hill, one of the most attractive parts of Hampstead, near the High Street. It was large and comfortably furnished, and Ithell lived there most of the year except for the periods when she stayed in her Cornish cottage. She was a good hostess, easy to talk to and with a good sense of humour, and we would sit surrounded by her paintings in the studio. These were mostly bleak landscapes, probably of Cornwall, the majority of which incorporated some sort of phallic symbol.

Ithell was unpretentious and on the surface appeared relatively conventional – although she sometimes wore a caftan – but we knew she had leanings towards the occult and that she had had some dealings with Aleister Crowley. (She once told me that Crowley had tried to seduce her and had chased her around his house.) We also knew that she had previously been married to an art historian and critic.

In the mid-1950s Ithell suggested to me that she write a travel book about Ireland, so I commissioned her to do so. The book, *The Crying of the Wind*, was distinctive and highly original, and Ithell supplied her own illustrations and designed the cover. The book, although unusual, sold reasonably well, and we followed it with *The Living Stones*, a book about Cornwall. Distinctly out of the ordinary, both books incorporated Ithell's interest in the occult and Celtic lore. However, partly because of Ithell's reminders, I couldn't get *Goose of Hermogenes* out of my mind, and in 1961 I decided to publish it. Yet again Ithell designed a very good cover, and the novel eventually sold out.

I had known that she was a painter of distinction but did not have a chance to see her earlier surrealist paintings until she had an exhibition at the Parkin Gallery in Sloane Square in the 1970s. This exhibition was an eye-opener for me; I came to the conclusion that her early work was her best. At any rate, it was a breakthrough for her, and on the strength of it the organizers sold Ithell's work on to major galleries.

By this time Ithell, who suffered from asthma, had, on her doctor's advice, moved permanently to Cornwall. After this Wendy and I saw very little of her, and the Parkin exhibition was the first time that I'd seen her in a long time – it turned out to be the last. She offered me a fine painting at a good price, but I stupidly did not take up her offer. This was, of course, an indication that there was not yet any great demand for her paintings, and it was only after her death in 1988 that real national and international regard for her work came about. I believe she was aware of her unusual ability and disappointed that she did not receive the recognition she deserved during her lifetime. But she was never bitter.

I miss Ithell. She was one of the few really brilliant and exceptionally talented people I ever met who was good company, genuinely unassuming and always a pleasure to be with.

Peter Owen, 2003

ITHELL COLQUHOUN (1906–88)
A Background to the Artist
by Eric Ratcliffe

It was in 1955 that, using his gift for selecting promising manuscripts, the independent publisher Peter Owen produced the first travel/biographical book by the surrealist artist Ithell Colquhoun. Entitled *The Crying of the Wind: Ireland*, it had been written following a trip she took with friends, travelling from Dublin up to the north-west coast of Ireland and back, taking in various detours *en route*. The travel element of the book was secondary to a descriptive feast of Irish lore and habits, ancient wells, fairy traditions and legends. She was obviously deeply attracted to these features of the landscape. The *Times Literary Supplement*, on 30 September 1955, referred to it as 'a rare and beautiful travel book' and mentioned the air of mystery that it exuded: 'Here is the authentic touch of the Gothic novelist, and one wishes that Miss Colquhoun had both the canvas large enough and the unrestricted scope to introduce the mysterious figures that should flit across this darkling landscape.'

This 'authentic touch' was to be fulfilled six years later, when Peter Owen published the first edition of *Goose of Hermogenes* in 1961. The manuscript had been completed some time previously, and its publication followed Colquhoun's second travel book, *The Living Stones: Cornwall*, published by Peter Owen in 1957, which had been inspired by the landscape surrounding a converted hut in the Lamorna Valley in Cornwall in which Ithell had lived and painted for a time before she moved along the coast to Paul, near Newlyn. It is with *The Living Stones* that we fully comprehend that Ithell Colquhoun regarded nature as she found it in the valley and on the cliffs beyond as a part of her, she as one with the flowers and birds – the long-tailed tits, the whistle of the goldcrest, the bluebells and the campion, the sea pinks along the cliffs: 'I am identified with every leaf and pebble, and any threatened hurt to the wilderness of the valley seems to me like a rape.'

Ithell Colquhoun's psychic sensitivity to nature cannot be over-emphasized. She was not simply romanticizing about her feeling of being magnetically attracted to the wonders she found in standing stones, circles, wells, the old saints and nature's life. It was a living landscape, not simply a backdrop for tourists or a means to an end for those who made their living from the land.

After a sound education at Cheltenham Ladies' College, where she had been noted as showing really good ability in 'humane subjects', Ithell had studied at the Slade School of Fine Art, being awarded the summer prize in 1929 for her painting *Judith Showing the Head of Holofernes*, which was shown at the Royal Academy exhibition in 1931.

From painting in a traditional mode during and immediately after a short period living in Paris in 1931, she began to work in a surrealist style, having become acquainted with the *Surrealist Manifesto* of André Breton and visiting exhibitions showing the work of Salvador Dalí. The year 1939 was one of peak painting activity for her and a time when she was getting recognition as a mature and skilful artist. However, in 1940 she was expelled from the London Surrealist Group, of which she had been a member for little more than one year, as she was unable to conform to the dictats of E.L.T. Mesens, as expounded in a meeting of the group on 11 April at the Barcelona restaurant in Soho. The main issue was that surrealists should refuse to participate in exhibitions springing from 'artistic bourgeois spirit'; other points were adherence to the proletarian revolution and a ban on joining secret societies. Ithell was unable to conform to the strictures imposed by Mesens and was thus expelled from the group.

Her dedication to her work as a rising and mature artist at the end of 1939 had resulted in her showing in twenty exhibitions (five of them solo), and as an independent she went on to participate in about a hundred more as her work became known and appreciated. She was never remembered as a celebrity name in surrealist painting, and her role as a pioneering woman surrealist painter in England has never been adequately acknowledged. It is reasonable to conclude that this must be ascribed to the 1939 expulsion and subsequent bias against her and her husband, the surrealist artist, critic and art historian Toni del Renzio, who was newly arrived in England and was looked on as an upstart attempting to redefine the path of surrealists there. Another factor was that, as her association with the group had not formally begun until 1938, she had missed being represented in the prestigious International Exhibition of 1936 at the New Burlington Galleries in London, the first full exhibition of surrealist works in Britain, and so her name was not associated with the surrealists in the public mind. Nevertheless, the couple's home in Bedford Park, west London, was a well-known venue for surrealists to gather in the early years of the Second World War.

She did receive a great deal of publicity from her solo exhibitions and the catalogues that accompanied them. Substantial information about her work, together with reproductions of it, can be found in *Surrealism in Britain* by Michel Remy and *Women Artists and the Surrealist Movement* by Whitney Chadwick.

Ithell's work in Cornwall, often employing automatic techniques, have a mystique no doubt stemming from the absorption of more esoteric knowledge, continuing an interest in the subject which began in the period around her early studies at the Slade. Her final book, published in 1975, *Sword of Wisdom: MacGregor Mathers and the Golden Dawn* (Neville Spearman, London), contains much of her accrued occult knowledge and theory.

She exhibited widely abroad and had two solo exhibitions, in West Berlin and Hamburg, as well as touring with the Fantasmagie group in Czechoslovakia. She wrote a great deal of poetry, some of which was collected in *Grimoire of the Entangled Thicket* (Ore Publications, Stevenage, 1973) and in *Osmazone* (Dunganon, Sweden, 1982).

The Hermogenes of the title – the name means 'born of Hermes' – was a Carthaginian philosopher-painter. He was contemporary with Tertullian – an early church father, also a Carthaginian – and his anti-Christian gnosticism provoked a long treatise from Tertullian, in which he likened the philosophy of Hermogenes to his bad painting. Within the terminological confusion of the medieval alchemists, the Goose of Hermogenes was one name for the elixir that was produced at the end of the Opus, the Philosopher's Stone itself. Was this the fabulous goose that laid the golden egg?

Each chapter in the *Goose* has a title relevant to a stage in the alchemical progression to complete the Opus, the Great Work. This short book appears to be an exceptionally sustained surrealist text. It is, with its moving and changing allegory, dream imagery set in a framework of the strange happenings that befall the narrator, a parade of the unconscious modified and made elegant by the skills of the author, indeed an opus in its own right. Read on.

The following galleries have acquired work by Ithell Colquhoun for public display:

Bradford, Cartwright Hall Gallery: *St Elmo* (pen, black ink, gouache, c. 1947)

Glasgow, Hunterian Art Gallery: *Gouffres Amers (Méditerranée)* (oil on canvas, 1939)

Government Art Collection: *Marlowe's Faust* (a scene from Christopher Marlowe's *Doctor Faustus*) (oil on canvas, 1931)

Hove Museum and Art Gallery: *Interior* (oil on board, 1939); *The Judgement of Paris* (oil on canvas, c. 1930)

Israel Museum, Jerusalem: *La Cathédrale Engloutie* (oil on canvas, 1952); *The Pine Family* (oil on canvas, 1941)

London, National Portrait Gallery: *Humfry Gilbert Garth Payne* (ink and watercolour, 1934); *Self-Portrait* (two) (both ink and watercolour, undated)

London, Tate Gallery: *Scylla* (oil on board, 1938)

Royal Cornwall Museum, Truro: *Dark Fire* (enamel on board, 1980), *Death of a Vampire* (oil on canvas, c. 1960); *Interior Landscape* (ink drawing, 1947); *Landscape with Antiquities, Lamorna* (oil on canvas, 1955); *Study of Shells* (1930) [All items on loan from the National Trust]

Southampton City Art Gallery: *Rivières Tièdes (Méditerranée)* (oil on wood, 1939)

To the Azores – unvisited islands

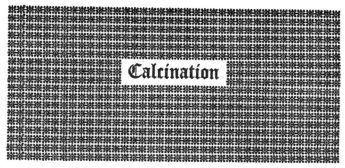

Calcination

'Thou still-unravished bride of quietness!' – Keats.

I think I must have been still in the erratic local bus when I first caught sight of my Uncle's island. It was situated in a misty bay almost land-locked by two promontories, and choked with a growth of the half-submerged trees, mostly a kind of willow. At the top of each tree sat a bird – missel-thrushes perhaps. But soon this faint landscape was hidden by the nearer of the two headlands, rocky and covered with vegetation, as the road turned inland from the coast.

I got out, found a horse and cart, and decided to approach the bay from the landward side. I started through the jungle, but soon the track became impassable for the cart; and after that even the horse had to be abandoned, for the way wound among great branches, over blocks of masonry and walls half-hidden under masses of dry grass, and beside patches of stagnant water where it finally petered out.

After climbing for some while through woodland slopes, I came to a curious house like a châlet,
with rustic woodwork round the stained-glass
windows – one of William Morris's enterprises, I
thought. I wanted to go inside and see the work
which was still, no doubt, being carried on there,
but a small faded woman approaching middle-age
appeared and discouraged me from entering. She
offered instead to show me the path to the bay,
which I had missed; but as we went forward she
behaved in an embarrassingly affectionate manner
towards me; however, I put up with that, as I
wanted to know the way. We came to a stile; I got
over first and tried to help her, but when she had
put her foot over the main part of it, she stepped
on a wooden bar the other side, which broke and
she fell. I helped her up, but she was rather dazed,
and seemed now to have little more idea of the
direction than I had myself. We wandered on for
some distance further, through country which,
though steep and overgrown, was yet more open
than that which I had passed through before, and
the air above it more easily pierced by the sun's rays.
We could hear the moaning of surf on rocks; and
presently came to something resembling a con-
structed wall, but built as it were against the hillside. Oblong pillars in bad repair marked an

entrance through it, and a rough path was visible beyond.

My companion explained to me, that two kinds of monks were to be seen in the vicinity, one kind dressed in brown and the other in brown and white. The domain had the appearance of a panorama, and we seemed to be looking at a painted scene of monks dining out of doors. At each end of the table sat a monk with wings. She told me that once a year, early in December, the convent was open to the public, and this being the day, we could go over it.

She led me up the monastery-garden-path to the building. We went in, up a stairway and along a corridor, where I came across a rosy-faced youth who was looking over the monastery. He pursued and caught me; I struggled. In the rough-and-tumble that followed we edged from the corridor into an empty room with a square unglazed window at the level of the floor. It looked down upon terrible rocks and sea below. Still struggling, we moved towards it and I pushed him through. But looking out after him, I saw only an empty shirt falling through the air.

I rejoined my guide in the passage, and we went on a little further; then I entered a small room to the right of the stairs. The walls were colour-washed sea-green like the rest of the monastery; the air within was very close, strongly scented with some

9

A*

exotic perfume and resonant with a strange humming. I fell at once into a kind of trance and sank down upon the floor. To the right of the door three women were sitting round a low table playing cards, and one was dealing with incredible speed. The cards were small, with backs of dark plain colours, red, green or brownish. Directly opposite me was a fourth woman, crouched upon the floor praying in front of some cult-objects – a bell, a censer, a bowl for offerings. This one was performing a rite which included rhythmical beats on an instrument something like a xylophone, but made with plates of metal instead of wood. All the women were of oriental appearance, Berbers from the mainland perhaps; their hair was plastered with some dark substance into a number of stringy locks; their garments were bluish. I was overcome by the extraordinary atmosphere of the room, which filled both mind and senses. I had left the door open and through it I could see my guide; and as she would not enter, I staggered to my feet and went out. Once outside, the symptoms of trance vanished and I could get my breath.

In one of the higher storeys was a large room with several monks sitting near the window. I went into the bathroom adjoining to wash my hands; the towel looked dirty. It is one of the monks' towels, I thought, it is not clean enough for me to use, they are not very particular. The monks were going to sing; they were quite sweet. Did they sing or did they wash their hands?

I cannot say, for we continued our journey, the precipitous coast somewhere at our backs, along the plain below the western ridge of the bay. My first glimpse was of the two windows in the top storey; they were sash-windows but the Gothic masonry of their outer surrounds gave the effect, if one did not look closely, of lancets. By the blackness of their cavities I thought the place untenanted.

As we moved, however, the intervening screen of spinney passed to one side, revealing a lower storey rising direct from the turf of the hillside. In the ground-floor two more windows presented themselves, larger than the upper ones. Over each a grey fluted canopy, something like the half-section of an onion-dome but more elongated, rose to a point between the attics. This next floor below was certainly lived in, for we could see through the open windows polished furniture, glass and mahogany, and portrait silhouettes on green or pinkish walls; and could hear a faint sound of music.

The house, being built into the hillside itself, seemed scarcely more than a façade; though how deeply the building caved into the earth at the back, one could not tell. At the sides, which seemed very

11

shallow, the stone of the structure merged into the steep downland turf.

We now saw that the whole façade was double, that in fact it reproduced itself less clearly to the left, the direction from which we had come. There was a kind of balcony running across the entire front; to the right it formed a small conservatory, and through this we passed. I noticed a tropical plant with finely cut leaves and large citron-coloured flowers like bells. We found ourselves in a corridor, dividing those rooms which opened upon the façade from certain others which gave upon the back, and led to a door at the far end, through which the legs of a man sitting in an easy chair were visible. There was a sound of distant conversation.

One of the rooms at the back was a spacious twilit kitchen and into this we glided. There was a basket on the dresser containing tongue-sandwiches and fruit. I took these and began to eat a sandwich. I wondered how we should explain our presence if anyone came.

'Leave it to me,' said my companion.

Footsteps approached; a slim dusky girl with cherry lips entered. My companion said this was Sylvia – the name seemed inevitable – and told her how we had been sent to take some measurements. Sylvia seemed quite satisfied with this explanation, but I began to improvise that we had been unable to come at the time stipulated. This remark carried less conviction and I thought I had better keep quiet. I was also embarrassed by the half-eaten sandwich that I was trying to finish, having replaced the rest of the food in the basket. We drifted about inconclusively for a little, my companion talking to Sylvia in confidential tones. Finally we were shown out through the back door, which gave upon a pebbly drive, not into the depths of the hillside as I should have expected.

This drive was set in a garden bounded by a low wall; sunlight filtered across its declivities through eucalyptus trees and many plants of the tamarisk tribe. In the middle of the drive was raised a flower-bed bordered with stones, and here had alighted the weight of a creature like certain parasitic orchids, though much larger. It had grey downy leaves, a body-hull and neck-mast-stems covered with woody scales; and starting from the tip of each stem, a crest-pennant of silky orange petals. Each scale was set, not pointing downwards as on the neck and body of a swan, but upwards. There it floated, becalmed in the soil like a boat on an oval pond; but the image of it followed me as we traversed the parklands.

We continued along the line of the wall to a distant point where it was low enough to climb, and came out upon the downs bordering the sea. My Uncle's island was again visible; but though I looked for it carefully I could not pick out his house. A village could be seen, backing a small harbour and its diminutive lighthouse; but further inland there was no sign of human habitation, only crags fit for the hawk and eagle. I knew that I should seek in the centre of the island, but all that appeared there was an immense concavity suggesting the crater of a volcano, perhaps not yet quite extinct.

We made our way downhill to a jetty where a coracle was tied. I said goodbye to the woman who had helped me to get thus far, with polite hopes that she would not miss the way back to her châlet. I had some difficulty in steering the flimsy boat between the willows, whose drooping lower branches soon hid my former companion from view. I think she waited for some time on the tiny mole, looking after me. 'Don't watch me out of sight!' I called. 'It's bad luck!'

But the myriad missel-thrushes, inspired by the sunset, were all singing at once, and I doubt if she heard me.

Solution

'Or was it then that a black cloud from heaven
Such blackness gave to your Nazarene's hair,
As of a languid willow by the river
Brooding in moonless night?' – Unamuno.

It was late evening when I arrived at my Uncle's house, after travelling away from the harbour so far that I judged I must be near the centre of the island. I could not be sure of the location of the demesne as regards the volcanic depression I had observed from the main island, because of the duskiness of my path, which wound through a stretch of coniferous woodland and allowed me no general view. I guessed, however, that the territory must lie somewhere along the eastern slopes of that central mountain.

I remained for my first night at the gate-house, a rectangular building which stood a little apart from the mansion itself. The only inhabitant was an Anchorite who acted as porter, but so few visitors

15

came this way that his devotions were seldom interrupted. He wore a black gown with a white cord knotted round the waist.

I gathered from this guardian a somewhat sinister impression of my Uncle, and of the house beyond. The Anchorite's relationship to them was evidently one of dependance – my Uncle had some hold over him which made of him a minion. Nevertheless his will was not entirely subjugated, and I had the impression that he wanted to convey to me some warning without, however, saying enough to compromise himself.

This impression was but deepened when he spoke, after a few minutes, at some length.

'I once had two beautiful exotic creatures,' he began, 'one dark, the other excessively blond, called the Crow-moth and the Moon-moth. Both were very large.

'The Moon-moth was perhaps the more striking in shape – its front wings were so curved as to be almost hooked and the hind wings had long swallowtails of delicate pink and yellow. The general colour was a pale green, emerald in hue but milky, with borderings and eye-markings of a slightly intenser yellow and an artificial-looking pink. These in their turn were emphasised by a very little deep maroon colour, the only colour of any strength in the design. The wing scales were fine and soft, and long silky

16

hair grew near the body. The antennae were branched and feathery. The flight might be swift, but it must always have in it something of the glide or the flutter.

'If the Moon-moth seemed to suggest the vertical, the Crow-moth with its long and narrow fore-wings stressed the horizontal. It was thick and heavy, and its flight, you felt, must be low and darting, though extremely powerful. The fore-wings were sooty black, the veins strongly marked with a powdering of silver scales, each one separately visible, and the hind-wings bright yellow with veins and borders of black. Each of the fore-wings, looked at by itself, might have been a single stiff feather. The body and wire-like antennae were black; I was always a little afraid of the Crow-moth. Did it mean death? and the Moon-moth, those insubstantial cravings after immortality?'

Before I could make any comment on this surprising monologue, the Anchorite turned away and passed noiselessly through the only door of the apartment, in order to tend, I almost fancied, the ethereal pets he had just described; though whether these were insects, sylphs or women, I could not from his manner be sure. Meanwhile I had little to do but look about me; and though I was not invited to enter other rooms, I knew that such there must certainly be, from the looming architectural mass that I had been able approximately to measure in the deep twilight outside.

Although the room in which I found myself was well-warmed and furnished, and brightly lit, these very comforts seemed to be arranged, not so much for their own sake, as for a defence against outer darkness – there was an atmosphere of the deliberately sequestered, and of something unobtrusively but constantly alert.

Next day I went on to the mansion which, though set apart from the gate-house, was not far distant. The plan of it was roughly a square surrounding, I imagine, a central courtyard, though this I never saw. It was large and illustriously furnished; and if somewhat crepuscular in lighting, was well kept by the self-effacing servants. From the main landing upstairs there led off two side corridors; the one to the right was short and gave directly upon my Uncle's own apartments, the other to the left was long and shadowy, and led I knew not where, though I fancied my Uncle's suite must have, at its extremity, another entrance giving upon it. In fact his rooms occupied a good half of the house, all that part to the right of the central courtyard, and also the part served by the unseen corridor which I imagined must run parallel with the main landing.

My first view of my Uncle was disquieting; I saw no sign of him until the evening when, after dark,

18

I noticed a slit of light beneath the door of his study. I would have entered, but the Anchorite, who suggested to me how to act in regard to my Uncle – and indeed saw to the general direction of the household – told me not to tap on the door, but to wait. After a few seconds a shutter, not unlike that of a box-office, opened in the middle of the panelling; and in this aperture, illumined from within by a glow faintly rose-coloured, appeared my Uncle's hands. They held a few leaves from some rare booklet, embossed and illuminated with half-perceived designs. The pages fluttered for a few moments like a butterfly on some fleshy exotic bloom, then the shutter was drawn again and the door darkened.

The following morning my Uncle appeared to me in one of the passages, coming upon me as if by hazard while I was passing from one part of the house to another. He was tall, with a white and skeletal head, and was garbed in a purple silk dressing-gown fastened at the neck with a large copper pin of interlaced workmanship. The Celtic design of this, his only ornament, made it seem like a genuine find, though I did not dare to question him about it. The whole remarkable *tenu* I soon discovered to be his habitual costume.

His manner was courteous but distant; he seemed to have no need of any human relationship, and to consider enquiries about my health or journey superfluous. (I understood that I was to take the strange peep-show I had witnessed the night before as an indication of welcome – that all was 'Open' and full of good-will. Indeed the Anchorite had been quite overawed by it and had indicated that I was highly favoured.)

'Do not be misled for a moment,' intoned my alarming relative, his figure towering hieratically above me into the shadows of the corridor, 'this place is not what at first sight it seems. Do not be deceived by the port, the strand, the square; nor cafés, hotels, cavernous shops, houses gaunt or gay; nor by the churches, soaring or sequestered. The real village is not there. But look inland, up the valley; there you will find among cypresses the more persistent counterpart, like a reservoir defended by a wall.

'Here we believe in giving the dead elbow-room; each tomb is the size of a small house, white or colour-washed, decorated with tracery of iron wire, mouldings, reliefs, and unfading flowers of beads. Over every front door is carved the name of the inhabiting family, which is a very practical idea, because these people never move house. No provision is made for business or pleasure, but only for endurance and contemplation.

'They told me that the village had been inundated by an enormous tidal wave and completely submerged. Then I heard that this was not so; there had indeed been a great flood, but the tower was only under water to the height of seventy-six feet. One of the streets, too, the one leading to the tower, was still dry; and I seemed to see its tawny colour, the result of centuries of dust. But memory had no part in this picture, for there was no such street or tower in the place I knew.'

His voice died away, the rhetorical *élan* of his opening lines having spent itself. I was impressed by his fluency, the more so, as I understood that he seldom spoke at all; but I was determined not to be outdone.

'What you say reminds me of some experiences of my own,' I began, my voice hurrying nervously forward. 'We were driving, a party of people, down a street in a poor and slummy quarter, "the lower end of the High Street." I paid particular attention to the shop-windows; their contents were not easy to catalogue, but they were somehow suggestive, and I remember thinking, such things would not be displayed in a more select neighbourhood. One shop on the left sold mostly masks, which I remember as white with red touches, vaguely sinister; another cards, with erotic messages and symbolic designs; also herbs, love-philtres, aphrodisiac books and prints; while one on the right showed coloured models and plaques in low relief. A friend drew my attention to one of these, a pinkish-red heart on a white ground surrounded by a band of blue; but the arrow, instead of piercing it, pointed upwards from it. He said it was a phallic symbol. One felt that there must be eerie brothels on nearly all these premises; the windows did not exhibit for sale, however, any fetish-garments, nor any of the more obvious accoutrements of the trade.

'At the end of the street we stopped. The windows of the shop which faced us were papered with magical and erotic prints; and I looked particularly at those covering the panes of the glass door, among which were two pencil-sketches, roughly done, of the traditional Shakti group.

'We went in and were greeted by Madame and a fair-haired young girl dressed in white with a blue sash. The place was furnished as a comfortable salon, and on a small table there was spread out before us a kind of chart about the size and consistency of a newspaper. I looked at it carefully and said, "This is based on the *Book of the Sacred Magic of Abramelin the Mage.*" Madame agreed, and seemed impressed by my knowledge. On the paper were some drawings and patches of printing which I connected by some chalk lines, and the pattern which resulted put me in mind of the Seal of Solomon.

'The chart became a board ruled with horizontal

and vertical lines and so divided into minute squares, variously coloured. Madame said to me, "Your destiny could be told by this." "Yes, if you had anyone who knew how to do it," I replied. "I have a woman but she is in one of the other rooms; I can call her if you like." I was doubtful of the woman's abilities. Then Madame said, "My daughter's destiny is figured here."

'Near each of the four corners there was a diagram; I don't recollect the two upper ones, but the one in the lower right hand corner represented the naked torso of a woman, only where the legs should be, was a conglomeration of those squares which were coloured red, and in place of the genitalia, a red shield on which was written in black, The Knave of Diamonds. I thought, Of course, this is the destiny of her daughter; but I said nothing.

'I had not then looked at the diagram in the left-hand corner, which was a larger agglomeration of black squares, with a black spot at the centre. "That is hell," someone said, and I thought, I might have suggested the other as her daughter's destiny, it wasn't the worst possible.

'I looked again carefully at the squares on the board, being anxious to arrange in my mind all the colours in their right order. "Black, Brown, Red, Pink, Buff, Yellow, White," I said, then saw that I had left out Mauve, and didn't know where to put it in.

'On the right-hand margin of the board I now noticed some compartments, divided from one another by cardboard partitions. I understood that these contained the materials for magical experiments; for in the centre was a long-shaped partition with a number of small phials, containing, I suppose, drugs and perfumes. Each phial was of a different colour and design, some perhaps astrological. One I remember was quite transparent, another black with a pair of silver wings, a third black with a white skull-and-cross-bones. The daughter began to demonstrate the uses of these phials to me, but our attention was soon distracted from the board and turned towards a show in a cyclorama against the wall opposite.

'This consisted of a proscenium, behind which was painted a sunset sky overarching a phantastic landscape of mountains and towers. In places, the towers seemed to be falling, while down through the mountains a broad road rushed like a river. As we feverishly followed this panoramic show, it came to me that this was the way to hell.'

Separation

*'Am I not a candidate for fame, to be heard
in the song
In Caer Pedryvan four times revolving!'*
                                                                    – Taliessin.

I seldom saw my Uncle except at meals; his habits
were elusive, yet I felt that none of my own movements went unnoticed by him, and that he had
methods of knowing all I did and thought. I had no
clear idea of how he occupied the greater part of his
time; but I had the impression that he was given
over to some obscure research or experiment, on
account of which he rarely left his rooms. His particular sanctum was referred to by the Anchorite
indifferently as 'study' or 'laboratory.' I somehow
guessed that my Uncle wanted me in his house
because of my jewels, which were beautiful as children's sweets and very precious, and which he probably fancied to be possessed of alchemystic powers.
But he had to obtain them from me by some not-

too-openly disreputable means, and this was not easy, since I always wore them.

One day I did not see my Uncle at all, for the weather being mild, I elected to spend the daylight hours in roaming about his extensive grounds. I say daylight, but the trees of the parkland were so grown with creepers and fungous mosses, that even at midday they cast a kind of diffused unnatural shade. I did not return till dusk and was let in by the Anchorite, whose manner was anxious and ill-at-ease. I gathered from his hints that my Uncle was displeased with me – that I had perhaps strayed too far from his influence, or lingered too near a part of the demesne which he would wish unvisited, and must therefore be regarded somewhat as a truant, or prodigal daughter. As I mounted the main stair-case and made towards my own rooms to change my clothes, I saw the light underneath my Uncle's door, and was going to knock; but the Anchorite restrained me, advising me not to try and see him before half-past nine, our usual dining-hour. With these indistinct warnings he glided away; but I paused for a moment by the door, and heard to my astonishment sounds like growls or groans coming from the other side of it. Not knowing what to do, and considerably scared, I retreated along the main landing and glanced down the left-hand corridor. At the far end I had a glimpse of my Uncle's draped figure before it passed noiselessly behind a curtained door. So faint was the apparition and so shadowy the air that I could be certain of nothing, not even if it were my Uncle, nor any being of human flesh and blood. But if indeed it were he, then the sounds I had heard from his study must have proceeded from some other creature, of whose existence I had been until then unaware.

At dinner I did not seek to explain how I had spent the day; nor did I attempt to hide my doings – that, I knew, would have been useless. Neither did my Uncle question me, for the good reason that he was already well-informed. Needless to say, our mutual confidence was not such that I could ask him about the sounds which had so much unnerved me a short while before. The meal passed off as usual, with reserve on both sides.

I had for some while suspected in my Uncle a faculty of relative omniscience – that is, an omniscience which extended to every person and thing contained in his demesne. Occasionally after I went to bed, and before I fell asleep, I was subject to a disagreeable sensation – as though someone were exploring me, not physically, but on some less palpable plane; or trying to influence me by acting directly upon my will, without the normal media of words or other suggestions. Once, the impression of psychic attack or invasion became so strong that I needed all my force to resist it. None the less, my will was instinctively bent on such resistance, since I felt that unless I succeeded in this, I should be irretrievably swept away. A kind of paralysis descended on my limbs as I fought; and so much energy was drained from my physical form that I found myself for some while unable to stir. But when it found me impenetrable, the influence left me and I could move again.

One night I must have felt the atmosphere of the house so oppressive that I went into the grounds and strolled about, instead of trying to rest. Or perhaps I had dozed off and begun to walk in my sleep; however that may be, I found myself outside the house though near it, in company with the Anchorite, concealed behind some bushes. I do not remember how I fell in with him; whether I had visited the gate-house, or found him also taking the night-air; or whether perhaps he had been set to watch and follow me. In any case, he was at my side, and we were both peering through the darkness at a shadowy figure. This was my Uncle, prowling through the shrubbery which flanked the opposite wing of the mansion; he carried a light which he showed from time to time, and seemed to be playing some strange game of Jack-o-lantern, either with himself or in the hope of attracting a phantom searcher. I felt sure, however, that he did not wish *me* to come and find him; and presently, a suspicion that he was observed began to agitate him, and he flashed his lantern here and there in the hope of discovering the spy. Then he began to mutter, and it seemed that from the darkness about him some companion replied; he next called out, but neither the Anchorite nor I answered a word. A beam from the lantern fell and remained directly upon the sparse bushes that protected us; it passed between their slender twigs and lighted up my hands. The Anchorite whispered to me to remain immobile; it seemed inevitable that my Uncle would see me, and be angered by my nocturnal roving and prying; but all at once he put out or covered the light, and passed on.

It was then that I became certain that he wanted my jewels; I was wearing rings and bracelets, and it was only by a miracle that the rays of the lamp had not glinted on their gold. The resolution came to me that I must leave his precincts; I turned to the Anchorite, and kissing the ends of his girdle in a gesture of farewell, I slipped away from him. For a moment a gleam from the fitful moon illumined the depth of his eyes, and he gave me a look which I could not interpret. Then I made off towards the gate-house. I had formulated no plan, but hoped that through pity or negligence he might have left open some way of escape.

Soon the dusky mass of the building loomed before me; I strained my eyes to see whether by any chance the heavy doors under the archway were parted and had ceased to bar my way to the world outside. Yes, a square patch of twilight appeared between their massive lintels; and as I came nearer I saw that both gates were drawn back, inviting me to freedom. I ran forward as if to embrace the universe; but found that I could not pass beyond the shadow of the walls. The same nightmarish immobility which I had experienced several times while in my room now weighted my limbs; but this time I could not even struggle, let alone resist successfully. I knew with a sickening sense of futility that my greatest efforts would be unequal to the power which imprisoned me. The open gates were a mockery; invisible barriers more powerful than any bolts of theirs restrained me from going through.

I could but turn away from the tantalizing prospect of a freedom which I might not achieve. Sauntering forlornly up the narrow avenue on my return to the mansion, my steps obscured by the shades of night as well as by a double line of sentinel firs, my foot struck an object lying in the centre of the pebbled way. It was a quarto volume, large but slim; and I am certain that it had not lain there on my outward path. I hastened towards a gap in the trees and waited impatiently for a lingering

30

veil of cirrus to bare the moon. The succeeding misty glimmer did not last more than a few minutes, and was only just strong enough to show me what I had found; but I could see that the book was bound in parchment, somewhat browned with age, and fastened with ribbons of a jaded rose-colour. There was no title on the outside, but when I opened it and turned a few leaves, I found that it was called *Corolla's Pinions*, and that it was not printed, but written out most carefully in a copper-plate hand. The unknown scribe must have used, I should think, a crow-quill dipped in sepia. The frontispiece was set out as a complete work, but I recognised it as a detail engraved from a painting, and traced this original to the grotesquely-beautiful *Garden of Delight* of Hieronymus Bosch. It consisted of that portion which represents a juicy stem balanced above a pool, and budding from its elaborate calyx, as of some bizarre growth, a globe of glass – scrying-crystal, medusan nacre, lunar milk-orb, prismatic bubble-film, who knows what? – that contains within it a promise of the future as personified flower-organs, the lover-twins. The boy and girl recline side by side on a bank, for the first time essaying together the touches of love. Their naked thighs already meet in a caress, but their slender hands and unslaked lips still hesitate before the votive titillations. These couching figures, scarcely differentiated as to sex, are utterly absorbed in one another; and they do not look outward from the amniotic sac, delicately-veined as a petal, which encloses them, though its transparency enables others to watch their nascent pleasure, which even on completion, will never discard its innocence.

I closed the book and hurried back to my room, where by the light of my candelabra, I glanced through a few paragraphs. I became rapidly engrossed, finding myself as completely identified with the heroine as though the story had been a record of my own past or future, and I now read every word.

Conjunction

'... it seemed that our two natures blent
Into a sphere from youthful sympathy;
Or else, to alter Plato's parable,
Into the white and yolk of the one shell.'

— *Yeats.*

Corolla's Pinions

On the occasion of the Duke's twenty-first birthday a large house-party had gathered for the week-end at the Hall, and it was thought that from among those invited the young Duke would choose a bride.

He was a delicate silverhaired boy who looked much younger than his years, for he had an ethereal face and the bones of a bird. He was an orphan; and his family in its wooded fortress of huge trees and oaken beams had been left, an inviolate island, by the Reformation untouched. He had been brought up by his Aunt Augusta, a large brown woman, now in the fifties, whose mouth would open to show formidable rows of yellow teeth. Everyone was nervous of her, including the family chaplain.

33

She wished to remain the sole guide of her young nephew's destiny, and, if the truth must be told, did not wish him to marry at all; but she recognised as clearly as anyone the importance of the line's continuance. This acknowledgement which she owed to posterity, and pressure from other quarters, had proved too strong even for her; and so it came about that many of the Duke's elderly collaterals had assembled round him, each with a protégée, to celebrate his coming-of-age, and to influence, if possible, his choice. The candidate whom Aunt Augusta looked on with least disfavour was a niece of hers, the Countess Astarte's daughter, a massive red-haired girl a year or two older than the Duke.

Corolla scarcely knew how it was that she came to be included in this rapacious gathering, since she had of herself no great position, and no one from among the elder generation to further her interests. Someone must, however, have obtained an invitation for her, perhaps simply as a courtesy due to cousins of the blood, however remote; or even partly on the ground of her sheer harmlessness and inability to rival more eligible young women.

What then must have been the general consternation, albeit wisely masked, when, on her being presented to the Duke Oriole, she was immediately marked out as his special favourite! From that moment he interested himself in no one else, and took no account of the elaborate festivities arranged in his honour, but evaded them whenever he could in order to wander off with her.

One hesitates to use the phrase 'love at first sight;' and not merely on account of its triteness, for the attenuated skein linking them was untouched by that tragic tension which, until this time at least, has always in the West been associated with romantic love. Indeed, it is doubtful whether even the Orient could provide a counterpart to this strange 'elective affinity;' though its origin may be sought in that hidden impact of the Levant on Europe, from which the Magian consciousness arises. Plato, perhaps, was looking eastward when he wrote of two beings contained in a single sphere to form a hermaphrodite whole, the androgynous egg. It seemed that Oriole and Corolla were in some sense the same person, a kind of Euphorion, and for this reason their link was without passion, a vegetative growth; or as if two clouds floating towards one another should coalesce – yet with something of apocalypse, as though mutually and for each, the other side of the moon were suddenly revealed. And since this was so, no intrigue however persistent, and no convention however strict, could finally keep them apart.

Corolla had not come to this visit primed with the well-defined ambitions of many of the other guests,

and had no thought of attempting to make herself
particularly alluring, still less of monopolising the
Duke's attention. Yet the bond of sympathy was immediately established between them; though she
could only guess at what formed it – whether the fact
that they were both orphans and both of the same
age, and that they shared some unexpected facial resemblance, had anything to do with it, she could
not tell. She only knew that when she saw him, his
rank and possessions meant nothing to her – she
forgot all about them; and would equally have forgotten their lack, had she met him, a forlorn beggar,
on some outlandish shore.

The celebrations at the Hall were not only social
in the strict sense but religious also, and on Sunday
morning the private chapel was full. Corolla sensed
a certain tension in the atmosphere which she could
neither define nor explain; Aunt Augusta seemed
to be in her most dictatorial mood; and an instance
occurred to justify the priest's apprehension of her,
for on his making a slight slip in the ritual, she
had no hesitation in loudly correcting him before
the assembled company. Cousin Alicia, also, gave
Corolla a very hard look as they were coming out
of the chapel; and this was one of the first intima-
tions she received that the Duke's preference for
her was not approved. She realised, of course, that
it could not have gone unremarked; no doubt there

36

had already been some gossiping in boudoirs; perhaps she had been branded as 'scheming' or 'a dark
horse', as the saying goes, when in fact she had done
nothing but flow unresisting with the tide of fate.
There may even have been established overnight
two rival camps – one composed of Alicia, her
mother the Countess Astarte and their supporters;
the other, of those, who, though envious of Alicia
yet had little chance themselves, and so were
inclined to side with Corolla against her from sheer
desperation.

Meanwhile, the companionship of Corolla had
become Oriole's chief delight, and they would roam
together for hours through his extensive grounds,
or go exploring in the ancient passages and chambers of his mighty mansion. Separate from the main
building, but not far away, was a church of fair size,
though not now in use, since the family preferred
the more convenient chapel which had recently
been built into the fabric of the house itself. The
interior of this abandoned fane was very beautiful,
and not neglected, but kept clean and in good
repair. Oriole particularly loved the place, as he
could be alone there to muse for hours without
being disturbed; and to Corolla he displayed en-
thusiastically all its beauties and curiosities, telling
her legends of the saints and heroes, many of them
connected with the family, whose images appeared

in stained-glass, carved wood or painted ceiling.

Some of the upper panes of the windows and the carvings in the roof could not be seen clearly from the ground, so Oriole proposed that they should fly up and look at them. Corolla demurred, thinking she would be unable to leave the floor, or would become giddy after a few feet; but Oriole said he would teach her. Hand in hand they rose into the air, through pallid beams of sunshine which poured across the spaces of the interior, gilding their suspended dust. It was with a sense of great elation that they floated about near the roof, examining its treasures one by one; but as Oriole was telling her the story of some coloured figure in the great east window, the young girl suddenly realised how far below her was the ground, and lost confidence in her power of being upborne. She began to tremble and lose her balance; but Oriole steadied her, and they sank to earth gently, hand in hand as they had risen.

It did not occur to Corolla as strange that they should be able to fly, though she dimly perceived that, had they demonstrated their power before the other guests, profound disquiet would have resulted. She felt that Oriole would not wish them to use this faculty unless they were by themselves; also, that it was perhaps primarily the intuition of such latent gift which had attracted him to her. It was a delightful secret between them; and after their first flight she knew that they were affianced.

However, her visit was by no means entirely filled with such enchanting episodes as this; as already related, by Sunday morning Corolla had begun to sense that her behaviour was being looked at askance, and by the afternoon she had definite proof of it. She was strolling in the garden, alone for the moment (though she had no doubt but that Oriole would soon join her) near some magnificent yew hedges fully twenty feet in height and almost as thick, when she heard, muffled by these multitudinous twigs and leaflets, the sound of voices.

'Come here, Oriole,' she heard Aunt Augusta say. 'There is something I want to tell you.'

'What is it, Aunt?' Oriole's crystalline voice responded. He did not wish to be delayed.

'My dear, I had rather you did not see too much of your cousin Corolla; you have other guests to consider, and she cannot be helpful to you.'

'But I must be with her, I like no one so much. She is quiet and makes me feel serene.'

'Listen to me, Oriole; this cannot continue. There is something you must know about her. A few years ago she was married secretly and has since been divorced in very shameful circumstances. She was living abroad at the time and I have only just heard the story from Aunt Astarte. Had I known of it before I should not, of course, have invited Corolla here.'

'I can't believe it,' was Oriole's stunned reply.

'It is true, none the less,' corroborated the voice of the Countess Astarte. 'The fact is, that though she masquerades as an innocent young girl, she is, I need hardly say, the very reverse.'

'Whatever she may have done since,' continued the voice of Aunt Augusta, 'she is still, according to our views, the wife of the man who married her; so I beg, Oriole, that however charming she seems, you will try to put all thought of her out of your mind. Her influence cannot be other than corrupting; and though, since she is our guest, we must be polite to her during the rest of her stay, we need not show her more than courtesy; and we must not expect to see her here again.'

'I understand,' replied Oriole, all the lustre gone from his voice. 'But please, Aunt Augusta, don't ask me to do anything or see anyone for an hour or so.'

While the two dowagers remained seated in an alcove of the yews, Oriole wandered sadly away. Corolla silently kept pace with his footsteps, following the line of the massive hedge, until a break occurred in its vegetal symmetry, when, taking the turning thus offered, she came upon him face to face.

'Oriole,' she cried in a reproachful tone, 'I heard all that your Aunt has just said to you, and I want to assure you that it is untrue. If she will not take my word, I can give her proof. But what hurts me far more than her injustice, is that even you seem to doubt me.'

'Then all those stories are lies?' he cried in relief.

'Yes, whatever their source. Decide for yourself what to do. I only want you to know that I have never been married, never even had a sweetheart, except you; and you, I think I have always known, though I did not meet you until two days ago.'

Oriole's face brightened.

'I knew I was not deceived!' he exclaimed. 'Nothing shall spoil our happiness now.'

They floated together like motes drawn by an aery tide in some celestial beam.

'Let's lie down here,' said Oriole, and hand in hand they sought a mossy incline which, sheltered with scented shrubs, made a rustic couch; and there they lay in tranced embrace, one cannot tell how long. Their dream was broken by a sound of retreating footsteps, and of voices in which were mingled anger and frustration. They knew that they had been not only seen but resentfully observed. They lay however a little longer; and then, walking with arms still entwined, returned to the Hall.

That evening their engagement was announced;

41

and when, next day, most of the other guests took
their leave, Oriole insisted that Corolla should
remain; should stay, indeed, until they could be
married. Aunt Augusta, though scarcely cordial, was
obliged to accept the situation with what grace she
could. She had even, since the outfacing of the
Countess Astarte, reacted a little in the young
orphan's favour.

Another and sadder consideration was the health
of the Duke, for the excitement of the last few days
seemed to have been more than his fragile constitu-
tion could bear. He now alternated between periods
of lassitude, in which, lying on a sofa, his hands
between Corolla's, he could do nothing but muse,
as they looked out from a lofty window on the
green and dusky stretches of the park; and bouts
of feverish coughing, in which he was ever bordering
on delirium. It soon became plain that the only
hope of saving his life, or even of prolonging it a
little, was to grant his every desire, chief of which
was, of course, his bride's constant presence. He
could not attend to the affairs of his vast estate, nor
had he any wish to do so; it was obvious that he
would never be able to assume the responsibilities
suitable to his rank, nor lead the life appropriate
to a wealthy and respected landowner. He was made
for an idyll, and beyond this his powers could not
reach.

One unforeseen result of Oriole's illness was the loss of his faculty of flight, so that his enchanting aery excursions with Corolla came to an end. This was a great grief to both, but more poignant perhaps to Corolla, since a veil, only half-transparent, had descended over Oriole, and his days and nights passed in a daze, now torpid, now lurid, which blurred the acuity of all his ideas and sensations. She did not care to fly alone, for it was an activity that, for her, would be incomplete without Oriole; nor did she have much opportunity to do so, even had she desired, since the patient was in constant need of her attentions.

But one evening when the weather was particularly cool and still, he grew more lucid and became almost as he had been when she first met him. She even had hope, as she sat beside him, her arm around his shoulders, of his complete recovery. His couch was placed close under a widely-opened window, from which they could look down upon the tranquil waters of a lake in the grounds, which darkly reflected its wooded nearer shores. This stretch of water wound in such a way as to look, from their viewpoint, almost like a river, and towards its far end the grassy verge was so low that there seemed little solid earth to divide the gleaming western clouds from their image in the mere.

Suddenly, from the air above, they heard a cry

that made them both start. It was like the call of
a bird, but sounding at the same time a note that
was almost human. They listened, and thought
they could discern a noise like the rhythmic
shuffle of enormous wings planing over the
mansion. They leaned out of the window and saw,
flying now above the middle of the lake, a bird in
shape like a swan, but so huge that it might have
been an albatross. The span of its wings showed
white against the shadowy woodlands; then as it
sank towards the furtherest water, it skimmed the
surface for a little, and came to rest, making a
closed silhouette on the double of the glowing sky.

Oriole had followed all the bird's movements
entranced; but it only floated in suspense, still as the
waters themselves, and seemed to be waiting. Suddenly, as though unknown to them some signal of
departure had been given, it rose into the empyrean,
spreading its magnificent pinions now against the
sunset.

Oriole had arisen trembling, and was climbing
out upon the window-sill. The sky's roseate reflec-
tion lent his pallid skin a glow almost of health,
and his eyes burned with excitement as he looked
back, inviting Corolla to follow him. Scrambling
out beside him, she took his hand as she had often
done before, and they launched themselves into the
air. This flight seemed even more easy and natural

44

than their previous ones, for they had not even to make the effort of ascension, being already far above the ground. They floated on, gently at first, then more rapidly so as not to lose sight of the bird. As they flew, leaving the mansion and its grounds far behind, they became permeated with light and colour; and their blood, always a single stream, now pulsed back and forth along the rays of the sun, as from some magnetic heart. The bird, too, must have felt a link with the fiery west, for it sailed on as though drawn without volition to plunge into that flaming core; and with this creature of air for guide, the two sailed effortlessly on, desiring no return.

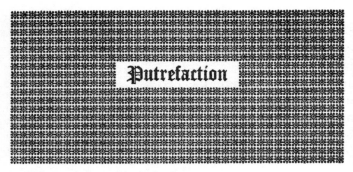

Putrefaction

'Blest night of wandering
In secret, where by none might I be spied,
Nor I see anything;
Without a light or guide,
Save that which in my heart burnt in my side.'
— *Saint John of the Cross.*

Tears flowed into my eyes, and this not only on
account of the delicate pathos of the tale. For the
first time since living in my Uncle's house, I wept.
Heaven knows, I had had enough disquieting experiences to puzzle and distress me, yet until this
moment I had only half-believed that they were true.
I had expected shortly to awake from a nightmare
—disagreeable enough while it lasted through the
day's earliest hours, but sure to flee at the first real
light of dawn. Now, however, the full significance
of my plight towered over me with dismal weight;
and a wave of utter loneliness overwhelmed me. I
realised that I was completely and, it seemed, permanently isolated from all help; with a frigidly-

tyrannous Uncle for sole companion, whose intentions towards me were certainly not benevolent, and the more disquieting because unknown. I was by this time convinced that he was mad; but I was none the less sure that he was possessed of powers beyond the common range, and this, perhaps just because he had deliberately pressed beyond the borders of sanity. I could not count on the presence of the Anchorite for friendly intervention, since his enigmatic caprices were hardly more consoling than the vagaries of my Uncle. What I longed for was a companion of my own age, someone discreet and sensitive in whom I could confide; in fact, for such a relationship as was described in the story. I longed above all for flight from my grievous present and for some such escape into well-being as that which the end of the romance, however mixed with poignancy, promised.

Too restless to sleep, I rose from my bed and went over to the open window, which gave upon a particularly sinister region of my Uncle's demesne.

Surrounded by spectral poplars there lay a choked-up mere, so thickly grown with rushes that the water was all but invisible. A low earthy dyke ran around it, and within this rim the dry ooze of its margin was spoored with the footprints of dinosaur and mastodon. Occasionally the rushes swayed and rustled with the movement of some huge sinuous creature and a strange cry might be heard, but whether of bird or animal one could not tell. The lineage of the spot could be traced in that most antique of plant-forms, the horsetail, which vied here with the suffocating rushes to obscure the pool. Once the horsetail, rich in silicon, grew as tall as now the poplars; to-day a vestige only of its pristine abundance, the jointed stems swayed in a smaller world.

This was a monstrous country—even the park-lands were alive with beings earlier than man. Tortured oak-trees stood or lay, piercing or hollow; a single ancient, near a Templars' site, reared a herd of ancestral horns and opened its side in a Gothick window. Does the Maiden sometimes look out? I wondered. Clumps of the druidic tree re-called that mysterious Nightingale who nested in nine oaks; the Russian 'Bylinay' sing of him, but whether he is bird or hero or demon they do not say.

Every copse was scarred by the passage of some tempestuous force: trees were torn up by the roots, limbs wrenched off, masses of twiglets crushed and broken. This destruction did not seem to be the work of any known wind, but rather of a sudden wanton downrush from the air, chaotic and convulsive.

Knuckles of flint broke as outcrops through the

soil of the rougher fields beyond, their shape echoing a goddess' torso or the curves of some unnamed beast. They seemed to be uncarved, but among them might there not be stones that the Templars treasured?

A feather like one of the primaries from a rook's wing much magnified was growing out of the landscape into the sky. The contrast between the quill, which was as thick as a tree-trunk, and the delicate branch-plumes that sprang from it, was terrible. A few of these plumes, chiefly the ones emerging near the base, were grey or whitish, reminding one of freak-blackbirds, frost, sere leaves, old age, and ultimately, I suppose, of dissolution.

The rest of the landscape was gay with the prismatic sheen of a thinly-veiled moon; and hilly fields hedged with clumps of woodland seem to invite me to walk among them. But how to avoid the feather? It dominated everything, and whichever way I turned my eye was led towards it, as if it were the magnetic north. What if one were drawn so close to it that one would have to touch it? The only consolation was the fact – I assumed it was a fact, though surrounding vegetation obscured my view – that the tip of the quill was buried in the earth, whitely, so that the most frightening part could not be seen.

Further away I noticed a goddess sitting cross-legged with her back to a cliff, the water at its base circling her loins. A passing giant smudged away her clavicles; her right breast detached itself, slithered down her torso, its tubular nipple pointing towards the lake, flopped in and melted. In its place appeared a great eye, lustrous as an owl's but clear-coloured like a bubble, surrounded with a foamy-white cornea. Her left breast remained some time, clinging to the surface of her ribs and shrinking gradually. It was finally washed away by a brief storm of thundery rain-drops; and the eye was put out by a flash of summer-lightning as if it had been pricked with a pin.

Alarmed by the seeming approach of a storm, I retreated from the window and again sought rest on the bed. I could hear no sound of thunder, but I sensed a tension in the atmosphere that might have but little to do with the weather outside. Was my room haunted? As an infant has difficulty in believing that it has left the womb, so a new ghost has difficulty in believing that it has left the world. Sometimes the ghost feels, acts, decides as though it were still blown-through by the breath of life. It has to remind itself constantly, and con-centrate its attention upon the fact that it is no longer alive: otherwise hauntings occur. Those ghosts return most persistently who have never

50

known that they were dead; others come back fitfully when they have known, and then again forgotten. When they fully realise it at last, their haunting ceases. A ghost must keep always before it a vision of that end which it has reached, and only allow itself to be worked on by the breath of death.

Certain ghosts feel little of that attraction of haunting which so powerfully influences many others, for these former leave upon the earth a physical manifestation in a human being. Sometimes this counterpart appears among their descendants; but when this is not so, another being is chosen and possessed, though perhaps this one is never wholly alien in a physical sense. The chosen one looks henceforth to the ghost as to an illustrious ancestor, and draws from it authority and inspiration.

The chosen being may be singled out in various ways, either before or after the death of the possessor. It may happen that those two halves of Plato's sphere cannot join on earth, but must be parted by a dividing dimension before they can work as one, the earth too narrow to hold them. One of them has to die. They struggle to decide which is to be the victim, and at last one of them kills the other. The survivor acts in self-defence, and there are thus many murders and suicides that go unrecognised by

51

law. But this being feels, mixed with pain and remorse, a subtle triumph, for it knows that from now onwards it drinks life at a double spring. That very identity which separated it from its inspirer during the day, at night draws them together. They are undivided but working in a manner both hidden and expressed, like an exoteric cult and the secret tradition which it both embodies and conceals. I am not here any longer, I am dead, it is only my unhappy ghost that wanders through my Uncle's mansion and demesne. I am lying in a small grave-yard at the edge of a thirsty plain, the dust is on my eyelids I cannot see, the earth is in my nostrils I cannot breathe, the pebbles are in my ears I cannot hear, the stones are on my feet I cannot move. We two have lain there a single corpse under rocky hills since the beginning of time, and one ghost is still walking, and one has ceased to walk.

I wonder how it was that I never lived in that room at the top of the house, the room with a large window and a view of the acropolis like a shout. Yes, like a shout I say—you could hear the triumphant noise it made striding upwards in the purple light. Why of course I remember now, someone else was living there, some tenant with a prior claim who did not want to leave. And then I was afraid that if I took that room I would go to Olympia with her and she would die there as she said she would if she

ever went back to her birthplace. And he dying
near by, dying in life, living in death, spending and
wasting and dying each time he was with me, each
time a step nearer death and death a thought dearer.
He was hungry once with that phosphorescent look
about him and asked to be kept alive and I gave
him stony gifts; I heaped those stones above him, I
laid him in that bed of boulders. We were held
together at last by slanderous bonds, by ridicule,
hatred, contempt, but there were older bonds than
those, the sulphur, the phosphor, the salt. Now lying
in a small graveyard near bones of kings and beaten
gold, he is learning the length of the horizon and
drawing perhaps where the worms twine a straighter
line than ever before; drawing perhaps the straight
wand of Hermes, with the snakes making spirals
around it to right and left, the red and the blue,
gyres that I must try to compas. Lying there far
from the shrine of a pillow he is echoing that distant
day when the first words he spoke were Listen to
me! And crying a far cry out of a six-foot cradle
he is saying again Listen!

I am listening O I am listening now at last I
have ears to hear.

An uneasy sleep must have drawn me into its
folds, for I awoke with a start. It had come to me
again, that dream; I thought it had visited me for
the last time. Then she is living still. What did

it say? that she was not dead, that it was strange how anyone could think so, how could the idea have arisen? As in the others, she had been away for a while—there had been no longer separation than that. There she was, smiling as in life; preparing to go away, collecting things together, I helping her. My true ancestor, the alchemists' white woman, lunar progenitrix—it seems that some ritual is wanting. What can I do? Mother of good counsel, help me; ark of the covenant, gate of heaven. It were not right ever to cease lamenting.

One of the most sinister emotions is hatred of the dead. Living, one has loved them; dead, one loves them for a while still more; then gradually one grows indifferent, and slowly one begins to hate. One conceals this as one never hides hatred of the living; their faults appear as in a beam of light, restricted but intense, that passes over a scarred surface. By this hatred one shares their death. It were not right ever to cease lamenting.

Some years after the tragedy, I found in the old Trocadero museum a massive panel of stone, which had been taken from the side of a tomb in Naples. It was carved in high relief with a Pietà, of the Romanesque style; but what devil had inspired the sculptor? A first glance assumed the traditional gestures of sorrow, but a second revealed the bodies of Saints and Virgin convulsed with a soundless and satanic laughter, their faces contorted with malicious joy. Even the mouth of the Christ, falling open in death, was pinched to an ironic smile; but most strange of all, the face of the Madonna was her face. It were not right ever to cease lamenting.

From a label near the ground I sought the name of the corpse thus commemorated; it was Agnès de Périgord, Empress of Byzantium, who had lived in the fourteenth century. The name conveyed little to me at the time, and later research has brought me little more. She was married to John of Gravina, Prince of Achaia, and by him had three sons. He died young, leaving her to the life of Naples' licentious court. Perhaps, if records still exist, one could trace resemblances here and there between the two histories, but my impression is that these are nowhere striking. It is in character rather than in destiny that their likeness, identity even, must lie. Was the sculpture designed before this titular Empress died? Did she even order such a monument to mark her remains? Or was there something in her character while yet living that inspired a subtle blasphemy after her death? The meagre details of her life do nothing to unveil the mystery of her tomb. It were not right ever to cease lamenting.

Did her spirit, after many wanderings perhaps, come to me from Byzance with a magian load? I remembered that the woman I knew had died unconsoled, the remnants of faith unsupported, culmination of many anguished days; that the new ghost was followed twelve hours later by blood, the blood of her husband's suicide. The last time I saw her, one of her eyes was closed: that evening she grew worse; suddenly, early the next day she said, I can't hear, I can't see; then fell unconscious and died alone, unanointed, unfed.

> *'It were not right ever to cease lamenting*
> *It was like the parting of day from night.'*

During the year before her death, the only one of her life in which I knew her, she was visited by several strange visions. In the month of December, one night between sleeping and waking, she saw the gate of heaven shining out of the surrounding darkness with a multitude of gem-like colours, which like a kaleidoscope changed their shapes as they glittered, yet left the structure of the gate unchanged. This vision lasted for many minutes before it faded away. In the next month she experienced a vivid linking of the senses when some words, spoken by her husband, appeared to her mind's eye before their sound reached her ears; they took the form of an iron grid interlaced with small ivy-leaves. In the month of June she saw, when in a dreamlike state, an image possessing both the force of reality and the charm of a picture: it was a maiden running, whom she called Atalanta, with dark hair streaming out behind in a point as her feet skimmed the tops of ilex-trees. Around her spread a snowy waste; behind her gray mountains were ranged against a sky faintly pink. Her filmy garments clung to her as she fled, her pale face straining forward, her eyes gazing outward persistently; one thinks of the old alchemical treatise called *Atalanta Fugiens*. The next vision or waking dream came to her about the same time, and concerned an appearance of the Magi moving in silhouette across a pale sky. In the same month, one hot afternoon as she lay resting, she saw me naked by her window in the guise of the goddess Saraswati holding the pose of the 'Lotus-seat', but with head turned over the left shoulder. This figure remained for several minutes, moving slightly like an animated statue. And nightly she would see four angelic beings round her bed, and had great joy in conversing with them, though in waking hours she kept no certain memory of their words. It were not right ever to cease lamenting.

For more than a year now I have had on my throat the mark of a vampire's tooth. Here at my Uncle's mansion, a bat flew in at my bedroom window, fluttered about a little and went out. Another night, some creature burst from the wall to the left of my bed and escaped by the window. I sensed rather than saw it, being only half-awakened, but it seemed to have the wings of a bat with a span of several feet. It were not right ever to cease lamenting.

When the ghost begins to quicken, as the poet says, confusion of the death-bed over, is it sent—where? My mind refuses to follow. But some time before these strange and tragic happenings, I myself on the borderland of sleep, once became aware of trees encircling a glen, and of mist drooping from a roof of boughs. Beyond them a wall, lying like a belt thrown down, with a black door of oak for a buckle, girdled a fold of ground with live stones, each one overspread with lichen. The wood of the door was carved with a garland of five apples, and three stone steps led up to it; I mounted these and the door opened. Within was the sloping orchard of Eden, red earth disguised as green; and beyond a tangle of apple-branches, the flames of hell rose with serene clamour; for in this garden the worm does not die. Under a tree with broad leaves a figure was standing; her hair was like steel wire red-hot, and one contour of her face and the breast-folds of her garment glowed. She was alone, and in her single and never-ending gesture was the peace of despair. It were not right ever to cease lamenting.

Now a negro was dancing, and the faster he danced, the wilder grew the hidden music. Suddenly as it grew louder still, his limbs began to expand

and he could touch the eight corners of the vast
room with head, finger or toe. His white draperies,
too, flowed out, unrolling from some compact centre
within themselves. As he spun and somersaulted, his
bones ceased to stiffen, his skin to bind, his muscles
came untied; gravity was abated, space negated,
volume grew fluid. But time danced on, to the
tempo of the music without source; and when this
music stopped, the negro shrank again to his usual
size. In an underground cave, shining warmly from
some hidden illumination, a line of swathed
dancers began to move, springing up and down on
the same spot with magnetic gesticulations. Their
leader passed along the lines with an iron whip,
lashing them like spinning-tops to make them dance
more fiercely. Up and down the line he strode,
more and more swiftly; and all at once, as his
strokes grew more potent, the dancers began to glow.
Then, as he reached each one in turn, they succes-
sively burst into flame. Leaping ever higher, these
human torches filled the low-roofed cavern with
their ardent rite; and finally left the floor, to circle,
a chorus of serene fire-balloons, near the ceiling.

Only when my guttering candles had extinguished
themselves one by one did I fall asleep.

Congelation

'*S'entrassi'ndru paradisu, santu, santu,*
E nun truvass' a tia, mi n'esciria.'
— *Serenade of Zicava.*

With the coming of the false dawn I awoke again,
and lay pondering anew my dismal situation. I came
at last to the conclusion that, while I could not
immediately escape from my Uncle's domain, I
would at least thoroughly explore it. This would not
only give me something definite with which to
occupy my time, but might even discover to me some
means of circumventing his plan of incarceration.
I determined that I would first acquaint myself
intimately with the lie of all my Uncle's land, and
subsequently disclose to myself even the most recon-
dite crannies of his mansion.

That morning I accordingly set out to traverse
that whole strip of the island which belonged to my
Uncle; and towards its western extremity I came to
a beautiful garden. The path that led up to it
through straggling plantations of olives was steep,

but when I reached the top a sense of peace rewarded me, a precious peace that must have withstood many invasions. This garden was well kept in all essentials, though it retained an air of going its own sweet way. On its approaches grew poinsettias with ragged flame-coloured quills; and the hedge bordering an avenue of dragon-trees was scattered over with the papery blue flowers of plumbago and with a few nameless trumpet-shaped blooms of tawny pink which had a surface like membrane. Further in, under some very dark leaves, I found one or two rare flowers shaped like a bell, and of so smooth a white that they looked like porcelain that had been painted with crimson and deep yellow within. There were bushes of hibiscus with flowers in all shades of pink, a shrub covered with scarlet cocks-combs, palms, cacti, the pads of a Barbary fig. There were oblong pools of water, full to the level of the lawn and spread over with dark blue water-lilies, jacarandas with silver bark and no leaves to disturb their mauve-blue sprays; a cactus in the rockery with a single yellow flower opening only by moonlight; the green-white hanging horns of the datura scenting the still and humid air. I wandered among banana plants, their leaves delicately green when first open, but afterwards easily torn, and tiny cream-coloured tubes laden with honey and almost hidden under huge fleshy bracts

61

of purple and Indian-red; and by Bird-of-Paradise plants with the same leaves, but slender wings of white and blue, sprouting from a glistening purple sheath. All these were taking in peace from the peaceful atmosphere and breathing it out again, consuming and renewing this 'soil of an Eden forgone.'

Against an ethereal sky the icy peak of the almost-extinct volcano was writing *Siempre, siempre,* again and again all day long in swiftly-fading steam above the garden.

Innocencio appeared between delicate stems and immense leaves; he was of that blond type which survives perhaps from some Gothic invasion: a skin that tans quickly because of an undercurrent of darkness, but eyes that reflect the sea, and hair that can't resist the sun – 'My hair is of three colours,' he told me proudly; and so it was, darkish at the roots, dust-coloured in the middle, straw-pale on the outer layer. He had the figure of the dancing faun but with something uncouth in hands and feet, the face of a faun but without spite, commingling the Classic and the Barbarian with acute appeal.

He was a very poor boy; his shirts were varied with an irregular openwork where threads had run, his bathing-slip was so much darned that the original wool scarcely held together, and even his best shoes were patched. But he took no account of wealth or poverty, education or ignorance, the cultured or the rustic – such distinctions did not exist for him. He had no fervid convictions, I am sure, on politics or religion, for he lived in a pre-social world, a world of the human primary. His strength was in a relation, simple and unabashed, to movement, light, sound and the elements, and in a dawning lyricism.

He said he was a sailor, showing me a document which I could not understand, but which may have been some kind of certificate. He had made several voyages, he even said he was a captain; sometimes he spoke of travel and of his desire to see Lisbon, London and New York, and Rio where one of his brothers lived. Would he ever see them? To him these places were legendary names, cities built again in the life of his phantasy.

He was the son of the gardener; he had three brothers and two sisters living – others were 'under the earth.' He could read, though not easily; but when he suggested that we went to bathe from a distant beach, I noticed that he took with him a translation of the Bible. After a plunge in the turbulent surf, he rushed out and threw himself on the blue shingle; then, his ears echoing with Atlantic thunder, lay poring over the calamitous visions of Isaiah. I turned to the Song of Songs and read a few verses aloud: Innocencio seemed delighted. Then each in turn we buried one another up to the neck in the dark volcanic grains of the shore, Innocencio telling me that they contained healing properties and would do me good.

'I want to marry you,' he said. 'We will live for ever in a little house by the sea.'

'I want a big house,' I said.

'I will give it you,' he cried.

How can one answer such promises? Innocencio's words were dreams.

'We will have some children with fair hair,' he went on. 'It would be lovely if you had some children.'

At the time I did not know what to say, but have often remembered Innocencio's dialect version of the song;

> *Palomita blanca reluciente estrella*
> *Mas chula y mas bella*
> *Qu'un blanco jasmin –*

I asked Innocencio about the crater I had seen from the mainland, and the snowy peak I could even now see.

'Yes,' he replied, 'Right in the middle of the island is a huge volcano, a real volcano, quite as active as Vesuvius or Stromboli. It is called the Bed of Empedocles, and the name is true of this mountain, and of no other. We try to keep its activities hidden; we don't often admit even its existence to anyone from the mainland or even the other islands. When you see a glow in the night sky and ask us what it is, we tell you it's a fire in the scrub. So it may be, and very likely the olive trees are burning too; but what has started the conflagration? We won't tell you anything about those seething underground cauldrons that threaten to break through at any moment, and occasionally do so!'

'What does the pharos say, out there at the end of the jetty?' I asked.

'It flashes a message all night through, long after every other lamp is out, but not a message of comfort. Keep away, it says, I am alight, but so is the mountain! Keep away from these dangerous shores. And from above the inland ranges, I shall be turned into blood, cries the moon; and the stars wide-eyed with terror sink back into their cavernous abyss.

'Last eruption the mountain burst like a Bank and flung millions of pieces of money high into the air. They were scattered over a wide area of the surrounding hills, and were eagerly searched for and gathered up by people from the villages. Many a mattress and stocking now bulges with that extraordinary gold. Such was the explosive force that a few coins fell even as far away as England.

'But one never knows what a volcano will do next, so it is best to say nothing about it.'

65

C

Innocencio wandered away, his forehead clouded, as so often his native peak, by the dark legends of his race. In the afternoon I went out again, hoping to see him, but could not find the peaceful garden. I was not far from it, though, for there was sea below me, and I knew that the garden lay near that part of the estate which included a strip of coastline edged with precipitous cliffs.

I was looking down on the beach; was it a festival, that so many people were about? It must be the day of the sea-sports; my eyes search the holiday crowd for Innocencio. Shall I recognize him in this dazzling light? There he is! No, it is someone a little like him. I look in other directions and then suddenly I see him; he is walking with one of his companions, and talking of the contest to come. He is ready for it, wearing his bathing-slip and bonnet. He does not see me.

I am on the cliff-tops of my Uncle's domain; it is getting towards evening, the wind has risen but there are no clouds, huge waves are crashing on the rocks below. Spectators are gathered on the opposite cliff, cut off from me by a chasm, and waiting for the chief event of the sports. Here are townspeople and their visitors, with a few rustics from the mountains inland. All at once a commotion stirs them: Innocencio comes in sight round the headland, pulling a boat with all his strength against

the heavy sea. Will he ever reach the bay? Time
after time a powerful undertow sweeps him outward. Then putting forth a supreme effort he rides
inshore on the back of a ninth wave and is flung
beyond the drag of the out-rushing water. He cannot
be seen for spray, but a scream of triumph goes up
from the watchers.

'It has never been done before!' someone shouts
in excitement, 'No one else has finished the course.
He has pulled all the way from Galva – how many
miles? – and in the teeth of a north-east gale!'

'Innocencio! Innocencio!'

The cries of the people soar higher than the
stormy tumult; he has put them above Galva of the
Grasshoppers, their rival port; Innocencio is their
hero for ever, and even the people of Galva will
praise him.

I look down into his boat, rocking now in a
sheltered inlet; he has brought from Galva where
his sister lives a trophy without price. In the distance
and through tears it looks like two little brown dolls,
one bigger than the other and lighter in colour;
then I see that they are shoes from the feet of his
sister's children, his elder sister whose name is future
and present and past. Are they made from walnut-
shells and the skin of mouse and mole? They prove
that his boat has been to Galva; they will always be
his greatest treasure.

67

I look now into the heart of Innocencio; below
the proud surf lie images of the perpetual terror of
earth and sea; first the twelve men he saw frozen
stiff in the stranded lifeboat; then more recently the
brothers from Lumio drowned in each other's clasp,
the one trying to save the other – dragged from
translucent depths, so fast were they locked that no
one could separate their last embrace and they were
buried in the same grave; and finally the corpse he
had seen half-eaten by worms at the cemetery. His
ribs still echo with the horror of their tawny hue.

I open my veins to the east I open the veins of my
arm with the cut of a sliver of silicon. Blood pours
out from the left flows out till it reaches the sea goes
on flowing pours inexhaustible through the inexhaustible sea without chafe or pause till it surrounds
the island a line veining marble a red line in the
green sea taut from my arm making a long arm to
his home circling the island a ribbon of stain in the
foam unmixing like a rusty chain to bind him in
binding his home so he never can go nor a boat's
prow cut through a crown renewed without end of
mercurial metal from far-away gap whence it flows
only his tooth could mend the gap whence it flows
only his tongue lick up the stream at its source only
his tooth and his tongue.

Cibation

'In the wood of wonder her fountain sings.'
The Magical Aphorisms of Eugenius Philalethes.

Next day I persuaded the Anchorite to come walking with me in the same neighbourhood. The coast-scenery was so fine that presently we stopped to look at it, gazing across a bay to the far side where a line of jagged cliffs rose against the horizon.

'A year or two ago,' said the Anchorite, 'a girl and I were walking along this road. There was a spring-tide, gone down very low, as it has to-day; and as we looked across at that rocky shoal in the distance, we saw the towers and spires of a Gothic cathedral rising above it. The tide had gone out so far that this cathedral, normally submerged, was plainly visible.'

While the Anchorite was speaking I looked out over the expanse of the bay, and could almost behold the faintly-discernible architecture that he described. Outlined against the sky, it appeared distinctly to the mind's eye at least; and I could

69

imagine that it had taken but little carving of the rocks from which it grew, to turn nature into art.

The Anchorite did not tell me who the girl was.

'Just where we are,' he went on, 'the coast is so formed that the water can't ebb as far as it does from the opposite side of the bay. It's about dead-low now, and as you can see, there are only two or three hundred yards of sand between the road and the water. Well, as I was telling you, we were staring at the cathedral, which is hardly ever uncovered, when a lady stepped out of the sea quite near us. She appeared just where the sand dividing us from the water was narrowest, that is, about opposite where we are now. She was tall and fair and dressed in a robe of yellow silk, the colour between orange and lemon. She came towards us, and we walked over the wet sand to meet her.'

My eyes had come back from across the bay and were now concentrated upon the waveless touch of the nearer sea and shore. I could all but see the yellow-clad figure standing at the water's edge; and it seemed to me that there must have been other of her people – sea-men and sea-women, with her or not far behind, though the Anchorite said nothing about them.

'She spoke to us,' he continued (and I could almost hear the sea-woman's voice), 'telling us her name was Vellanserga, and inviting us to go with her into the cathedral. I refused; but the girl went, and was never heard of again.'

I knew that if the same invitation had been offered to me, I too would have accepted; and it showed how completely the Anchorite's movements were in subjection to my Uncle's service, that he had not done so.

Seeing that I was engrossed in meditation on his tale, the Anchorite withdrew.

Storm is in the air, but distant. Does it echo, or threaten? Is the air weighted by the melancholy of a tempest subsiding, or the anxious hush that precedes its first assault?

On the sea floats a head in profile, of heroic traits, a collar of violets encircling the severed neck. The flaxen hair, once looped-up, is now spread upon a watery surface, and tilted by recurring small waves. Some distant storm, surely, tore this head from a ship's prow; and the wood still bleeds, oozing a purple growth.

The salty taste of blood, I mused, comes from the sea, which being without colour, reflects a tint from the air above while turning its red globes into sea-anemones; but blood has kept these as a dye.

Here is the end of the land and the beginning of a country under the sea; an impalpable region stretches over the last of the earth and extends a long way under water. It is said that our starvation

is their plenty; that in time of war here, down there
reigns the deepest peace.

In a douce air above stones and soil, one is not
alone; mist is blown out towards a silvered horizon,
nothing perishes. Sometimes there is a thickening,
and a growing menace.

Round coastal rocks flows a true water, the
authentic Atlantide. It is not the peacock that
divides two continents, shrill-voiced but never terrible; nor that narrow and more deceptive iris
strait; nor yet the electric blue sweeping from
Teneriffe to Tory, though a swish from the tail of
the same dragon.

Under granite the saints lie buried; here a monument measured to human form still stands, there a
tree takes shape from the bones beneath, an honour-
able vessel. In yet earlier rock there pulses an
ancient sensual life, but the saints must be roused
up first. Their diadems are bright with Sunday
flowers, already they lift head and shoulders from
their covering slabs. When they come alive and walk
their own realm, the kingdom of vegetation, then
blood of beasts must warm the older stones and
power will wake from a deeper cave.

Men must be sacrificed then, but those who feed
upon them do not want their flesh – they are eaters
of dreams. The powers of the sky are hungry and

72

only men can fill them. They desire the direction of their four main streams.

I turn inland, not noticing where I go, and come suddenly upon a structure, half barn, half grotto, peopled with a pallid statuary, relict of ancient prows. Immediately before me rises a tall figure, a great woman, full Hesper, water in the curves of her heavy hair, in the massive folds of her clothing, in the acanthus-like foliage of the scrolls that support her – a wave breaking into leaf. Her eyes, hypnotised by the pole-star, see further than eyes with sight, for they meet both sky and ocean, empty of all but the moment that endures. Her gaze is intent upon an ever receding horizon, her posture stretches towards a region impossibly remote, an undiscoverable time. She is the type of the hero-woman, both mother and warrior, debased long since as Britannia, but stemming from the ancient line of foundered Atlantis.

Here in a sea-Valhalla, its walls encrusted with shells, are found her sisters; many are not heads merely, but forward-straining bodies too, mightily draped. All have a family resemblance, all reflect our sea-mother's noble features.

Before one of them, the seared amazon of antiquity comes to mind, for hazard has shorn away one of her breasts, and the scar is whitened now like the rest of her body by recent painting. Another figure,

73

the central one of the tableau, seems ready to take flight from between two carved winds who, crouching to her left and right on a throne of cloud, blow from distended cheeks, while above her hangs a frieze of lightning and cumulus. Some are fully-coloured, some altogether whitened, some white with faded washes of colour or traces of gold. Their dress recalls that of the queens on playing-cards, four directresses of destiny armed and resplendent. Some touch heart or brow with a rose, petals that resist both wind and tide. If it were not for the small feet or sometimes the shoulders – echo of mermaid-torso – which hold these figures of adventure back, attaching them to object and present – that unseen ship which yet moves, sways with the flux, disintegrated though seemingly solid – they would dash onwards in unending foam-like career. Head tossed upward, neck outstretched, and breast swelling with a double air – the lung's breath and the oncoming breeze – all declare it. What vision has parted these eyelids, fixed these pupils, carved these smiles of ecstacy, dishevelled these massive tresses, filled these bosoms, bent these spines like a bow, frozen this whole?

The sea's voice, almost out of earshot, is heard only as in the ear of a shell; and the sole water visible is an oblong tank, clear but black, which reflects a pod-like column bursting with strange fruit and unconcealing leaves. The women, their backs to the sea, look now towards that garden where trumpet-flowers and tree-lobelias remind them of some exotic shore.

But I have explored it already, and though the other day I could not find it when I looked for it, to-day I have no desire to enter. Still bemused by the gaze of the statue-woman, I cannot but search for her everywhere; and I find her in the land's own long memory.

She overthrew the Norsemen, she melted the Romans down. It was she who led the people. She fought on the hill of stones, she wore the tunic of battle, she wielded the sword, she rode. A breast-plate of stone and glass covers her egg-ribs; and it is said that small living creatures dwell within, but she can scarcely comprehend their gnat-like life.

Vellanserga weeps, her valley fills. She comes from the land-under-wave remembering the summer fires lighted in her honour and her train of young worshippers, girls and boys with fiery hair. But at full moon she is delighted; stone maidens wake and dance, notes jet from two or three giant pipes to the south-east somewhere by her knees, and from the north-west near her elbows are answered. Her bones become flutes. On the anniversary of her feast she stirs, sighs, half turns over, struggles to awake.

At the dark of every moon Vellanserga bleeds.

Her quick is hidden by a cloven bud overgrown with root-like tendrils, strawberry-red like a huge rose-gall; and by day an intoxicant juice is exuded drop by drop from the grotte below. Above the bush of rootlets a stem pushes up, with numbers of small tassels sprouting from it like greenish flowers, and by night this wick gives out an incandescent vapour – the colonist surmounting her left shoulder sees a distant glow in the hollow – and the organs are shaded by canopies of enormous leaves, each six-feet square and supported on a stalk scattered over with red barbs.

On a flat space of ground an oblong is marked out with sticks and a cord, a sacred enclosure. Phantom walls arise; her daughter dances there with a dark acrobat in magnetic embrace. Impalpable wires swing them out to the planets, cords and poles hang through space; and now, their breast-bones touching, they glide in the air, their limbs' action springing from a single centre. On paths drawn by the sea-gull they plunge and sway.

The other daughter goes down to a beach made of broken shells; what strange light is there, it is neither day nor night. The sea is calm, stretches away; on the wet sand there stands the skeleton of a tower. A few scaffold-poles rise upward, and others are held across them with rope. They wait. She calls to the king of fishes.

Cibation

On the slope of Vellanserga's right thigh a ghost
sometimes appears painfully at dusk, and horses
shy on one of her arterial roads. Down the middle
of her body goes a slim furrow furred with shrubs,
marking the course of her stream towards the sea.
Her navel is a pool of water-lilies; from her armpit
evening-primroses sprout. On the haunted bend by
the mill is shown the sanctuary where she lived as
a saint, and on her demesne are found other view-
cells and a healing well. Vellanserga sleeps; the
thickening of her coma is mist.

From her left side juts one of her ribs, a headed
stone; on the front is sketched a cross, on the back
an indecipherable poem in ogham is inscribed. This
marks the entrance to her chapel, now only foun-
dations. Ferns cover the mouldered walls, a single
column remains at the centre. The east is wanting
the pelvic arch, the white egg-cell, the lamp-
ichor; north and south lack aromatic fume and the
candles' waxen glow.

77

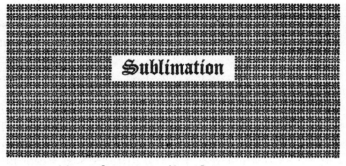

Sublimation

'Ou cela que furibond faute
De quelque perdition haute
Tout l'abîme vain éployé
Dans le si blanc cheveu qui traine
Avarement aura noyé
Le flanc enfant d'une sirène.'
— *Mallarmé.*

Back at the mansion, I determined to explore more fully the interior of my Uncle's domain; and accordingly I approached the door of the study through which, on my first evening, I had been vouchsafed the spectacle of the illuminated hands. To my surprise, the door was now slightly ajar; I pushed it open and found myself in what was no more than an ante-room giving, to the left, upon a series of chambers which housed the exhibits of a museum, and to the right, upon the immense dusky cavern of my Uncle's library. I say 'dusky', and this indeed was the impression it made upon me; yet it was by no means ill-lighted, and the areas at

78

window-level were furnished with books well-bound in, seemingly, the latest editions. It was further up, on the shelves above the windows, that shadow and festooning cobweb combined to hide a tattered array of volumes; while higher still, the rafters of the soaring roof were draped in utter darkness, and the forbidding antiquity of the treatises here stored formed but a screen for the flitter-mouse's crannies. These upper shelves were reached by an occasional rickety ladder leaned against the wall; and temerity bade me climb, but only about half-way, up one of these.

I began to examine the titles now ranged level with my eyes, such as *El Arte de los Metales* of Barba, *Anima Magica Abscondita, Coelum Terrae* and several other of the mystical essays of Thomas Vaughan including – ironically enough, considering the place in which I found it – *Aula Lucis.* Not far away were *The Open Entrance to the Closed Palace of the King* of Eirenaeus Philalethes, with *A Brief Guide to the Celestial Ruby* and *The Fount of Chemical Light* by the same author; while further on I discovered *The Golden Age Restored* of Henry Madathanas, *A New Pearl of Great Price* and *The Sophic Hydrolith.* But most of all it was the enigmatic *Book of Lambspring* by Nicholas Barnaud Delphinas that held my attention; and as I turned over its emblem-engraved leaves, a few pages of

manuscript fell out, written in a crabbed hand I
could only suppose my Uncle's. I had set myself to
lay open all I might of his secret researches, and
accordingly had no hesitation in scrutinising the
papers before me. This is what I read:

'Everything found on land is found in the sea.'

'Is it not time to break through that dismal convention of the scientific periodicals which orders,
however suavely, that only the driest language be
used? One would hardly know that these people were
making discoveries from the way they have to write
them up. Their particular kind of good form
decrees that every experiment, no matter how
dramatically successful, should be tabulated with
less symptom of personal zest than the pages of a
ledger can show.

'I have been able to observe some remarkable
facts about plant-life, hitherto unnoticed, particularly with regard to habitat; and I expect other
biologists to give these investigations their due, despite their unusual guise and staging. Indeed I hope
the more orthodox savants may even recognise here
a certain justice, since the things I am going to describe seem like sports of nature; though who knows?
further research may prove them to be instances of
some law previously unknown.

Experiment I.

'As I was climbing over the rocky ridges of a

valley I came upon a wide fissure slanting down towards the centre of the earth. I looked in and found
that its distant floor was water. I began to climb
down inside, taking hold of a natural bannister here,
stepping on an unhewn stair-tread there, which the
uneven surfaces provided. This descent was not
easy, as the rock was green with damp and patched
with a viscous wine-coloured growth.

'I had now penetrated to a vertiginous depth; if
I looked upward, the walls rose above me in a cool
shaft; turning downward, I could see a cave filled
with water the colour of crysolite, illumined from
some hidden source and darkened where a turn of
wall or jutting rock threw a shadow. One such submerged projection hid the mouth of the cave, making it invisible from the surface of the ground.

'I noticed that the water was not tideless, for it
began to sink with gurgling sounds, and in its
retreat left the cave without light. The rhythm of
this tide was very rapid, for scarcely had the cavern
been emptied, when the water came lapping back,
bringing the light with it. I tasted the water and
found it salt; and being unable to explore the cave
further because of its swift return, I began to climb
back towards the earth's surface. The going was still
more difficult than before, as I now discovered fish-
like flowers growing directly from the stone without
leaves. I could hardly get foot-hold or hand-hold

without crushing or gripping these cold petals, which spread their cherry and blue-grey all about the ascent, a salty deposit covering them with a dusty grape-like bloom.

Experiment II.

'It is not generally known, and certainly I never before this realised, that scattered about even the most cancerously-urban districts of great cities, there exist patches and stretches of wild marshy land or heath. I do not mean the parks – they are as urban as the buildings. These spaces are different because you cannot find them by looking for them – at least it seems to be so, as far as our present knowledge takes us.

'The other day when I was with a companion I found such a patch – a rough tussocky piece of land, quite extensive, where flowers of a unique and curious species were growing. The petals were large and looked as if they were made of paper – more like sepals, rather stiff and pointed; the colour was pale orange-pink at the edges, deepening further in and finally becoming a dusky reddish-brown at the centre.

'They grew in swampy places and we had to get wet in order to come close to them; we had to climb over rocks, too, and I was annoyed by my companion's lack of adventure in these matters – the way he jumped over the rock-pools you would think a drop of water would kill him. But I did not care; I made my way over the stones and streams to one of the biggest flowers.

'I found that inside and below the petals was a kind of bowl made of the same stuff; but it must have been stronger, because when I lifted the petals I saw that it was full to the brim with dark water. In this water were strange living creatures, like sea-anemones but larger and harder and without tentacles – more like scarabs perhaps. They were of various jewel-colours, ruby, sapphire, emerald, some of them spotted with white. They crawled and clung to the sides of the pool; I put my hand in and touched them, but my companion seemed afraid to. Then we turned northwards across the moor.

Experiment III.

'Another day I was looking for somewhere to live and went in a north-westerly direction. From some dingy agent in the vicinity I got the key of a house to let. Wandering along the streets I came to a row of peeling stucco houses with cat-walks in front, and mouldering urns, which could hold nothing, surmounting their plastered gate-posts.

'My key fitted the front door of one of these houses; I went in and up the stairs to the first floor. I entered a large room with three windows looking out upon the road; folding doors connected it with the room behind. These I pushed open and found myself in another room exactly like the first; I went over to the central one of its three windows and looked out. Instead of the characterless gardens and hinder façade of a parallel block, I saw a sloping strip of ground overgrown with brambles, then a pebbly shore, and beyond, the crash and smother of Atlantic waves, breaking ceaselessly and without tide. This ocean stretched away to the horizon where it met a misty sky, but did not merge with it – the heaving water set up a melancholy distinction out there; and here within, a briney exultant smell penetrated the panes, cutting through the mustiness of a house long closed.

'What extraordinary growths, I wondered, flowered in those wasteful depths? There must be a submerged garden whose silken green held curiosities far surpassing those I had come upon before. Idiots often visit such places and describe what they see; making idiots is one of the sea's favourite games. But when it tires of this from time to time, it casts up instead a supernatural being on an unwelcoming strand, who ever afterwards, spends his nights asleep at the bottom of some vast watery gulf.'

*   *   *

These notes belonged I imagined, to an early period in my Uncle's explorations when he was chiefly addicted to the study of plant-life, and before

84

he had buried himself in his island retreat. Now, I had reason to believe that the direction of his interests had changed.

There followed several pages of recipes, ranging from 'How to make a white milkie substance from the Raies of the Moon,' to the most gruesome instructions for the fabrication of the Homunculus. I was dismayed at this fanaticism, which made such a disagreeable impression on me that I hardly knew how to continue my investigations.

I was now convinced that his ultimate aim was the conquest of death itself; and to this end he would undertake no matter what, from experiments apparently the most trivial, and certainly innocuous, to those involving the final extremes of complexity and ruthlessness. To this pursuit he must have devoted many years; and I could not but feel an unwilling pity for one who, so palpably nearing the grave, was yet driven to spend his last energies in a futile attempt to evade it.

From my delvings in the library I gathered that he had already approached the problem from numerous angles; but that at the time of his invitation to me, it was the transcendental aspect of alchemystic philosophy that principally engaged his thought and practice. No doubt he believed that my jewels, many of which were heirlooms of ancient and wonderful design, could provide some link in his quest for the hidden nature of gems and precious metals, and ultimately, perhaps, for that Medicine of Metals which is the elixir of life itself. What more he fancied I cannot say, but I would set no limit to the bizarre dreams that may have whirled through his mind in its frenetic race with time. He may have speculated as to whether part of my jewellery was not made of alchemical gold, or a particular piece even contain the very Lapis Philosophorum; or yet again, whether I myself could not somehow be made the focus of unknown power and knowledge, and act as a burning-glass through which might stream some insufferable light.

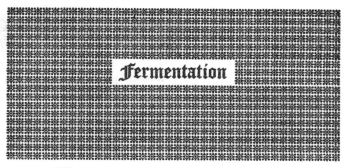

Fermentation

'Un no rompido sueño –
Un dia puro – allegre – libre
Quiero –
Libre de amor – de zelo
De odio – de esperanza – de rezelo.'
– Luis Ponce de Leon.

In one of my evening conversations with the
Anchorite, he suggested to me a walk in a direction
I had not hitherto essayed, and described a half-
ruined homestead, all that remained of an ancient
manor, whose architectural peculiarities he thought
might interest me. At least, this was the reason he
gave for the projected excursion to Troubh, but I
could never be sure that his simplest remarks did
not conceal a double intention. As he declared that
it was impossible for him to accompany me, I had
no choice but to discover for myself whatever was
hidden; and accordingly set out alone the next
afternoon. Something in his evasive manner as he
bade me Goodbye, caused me to wonder whether it

was against my Uncle's wishes that he had given me any directions at all.

It was towards evening when, after a long and exhausting walk, I at last came within sight of the lonely barton of Troubh. Owing to the undulating nature of the country, I had not been able to catch even a glimpse of the buildings from a distance; and now, massed around as they were by immense elms, I could see only a cornice here and a gate there, half hidden 'by the branches.

As I hurried along the wide pathway – it could hardly be so formally styled as 'avenue' – that led deviously towards the mouldering walls, more of the edifice revealed itself by degrees. It seemed to be very ancient – part-manor, part-farmhouse; and something in the architecture of the house itself, and of the various barns and stables surrounding it, made me think that at one time the whole place had been fortified. Now, however, there was not even a trace of habitation, let alone of readiness to receive, whether enemy or friend. The entire farmstead seemed to be given over to rook and jackdaw, whose strident calls filled the chilly gold of the sky.

I approached the front door and knocked. As I waited, full of curiosity as to what manner of being might open it, I determined that should my reception prove unsympathetic, I would merely say that I had lost my way and demand re-direction.

What was my surprise and delight, then, a few minutes later, when the door was opened by my beloved sister Victorina!

'Darling!' I cried, enraptured, flinging myself into her arms, 'how is it you are so near? And I did not know.'

'And how is it you are here?' she answered, equally astonished, though not so overjoyed. 'I thought you at least were safe,' she added, kissing me quietly.

'Safe?' I protested, 'I am almost a prisoner; and very lonely without the rest of you. Where are the others?'

'Hush, not so many questions: we are all within,' she whispered, drawing me indoors. 'You must stay here for the night; darkness will fall now before you can return.'

I was puzzled by Victorina's manner, for though she was pleased to see me, she seemed so pre-occupied with disquieting thoughts as to be almost disconcerted by my arrival. When I asked her to explain her presence here and above all her strange manner, her replies were far from reassuring.

It appeared that immediately after my departure from home on a visit to my Uncle, my mother had arranged to take this desolate country house on the same island, but did not wish me to be told of the plan. After mysterious negotiations, she had finally

installed herself here a few days since, with my four
sisters and my half-brother Rohan. If I had man-
aged to return to our old home on the main island,
I should have found it a habitation of spiders.

'I am sleeping in the haunted wing to-night,' said
Victorina. 'We take it in turns. You will not mind
sharing it with me?'

'No,' I answered. 'I shall not be afraid with you;'
and I really felt that my elder sister would be a pro-
tection against whatever 'the night side of nature'
might produce.

Nevertheless, the hours of darkness did not pass
peacefully for me, since I could not keep my attention from the creaks, sighs and sounds as of footsteps which nightly exude from the walls and furnishings of a chamber long disused. Victorina and I
occupied two biggish rooms with a communicating
door and a double bed in each. My windows looked
upon the garden, and moonlight would have poured
through them had I not taken the precaution of cur-
taining them closely. Even so, certain phosphorescent shafts contrived to penetrate them by sliding in between the edges of the blinds and window-
frames, and above the pelmets. Victorina's room
gave on to a deserted roadway at the back of the
house, and so was darker.

The disturbances seemed to come from the contents of my own room; but next morning Victorina

also complained of sleep disturbed, and by much more definite manifestations. Three times during the shadowed hours had she been aroused from her dozing by a visitant who had lain down beside her; and after a few minutes had vanished as unaccountably as he had come. I planned, therefore, to lie the next night across my bed rather than along it in order, as I hoped, to discourage similar attentions.

During the morning I gathered that my mother had found some means of informing my Uncle of my whereabouts; how this news was conveyed to him I cannot say, though I guessed that the Anchorite had been questioned when I was missing, and sent upon an unwilling errand. I more than suspected, however, that my mother and my Uncle shared the telepathic faculty which I mentioned before, and that by putting into practice certain techniques, were able to communicate with one another at will. There had always been an unnatural link between them as long as I could remember, a bond much closer than had ever existed between my mother and father. A suspicion that had long troubled the background of my mind now forced itself into consciousness.

On the day that ensued, my youngest sister Angelica, a frail dark-haired girl with the face of a changeling, was taken seriously ill. Our mother called in the doctor, but my sisters and I did not like him. He was a youngish, sandy-coloured man with nothing especially sinister in his appearance, but we all sensed that he was associated in some way with the hauntings, and we distrusted him, feeling that his ministrations could do Angelica no good.

The invalid's room also opened out from mine, but at right-angles to Victorina's and so was not, strictly speaking, to be included in the haunted wing. It was in close proximity, though, for as well as by a door, the connecting-wall was pierced by a window; but this was so thickly covered with white-wash that one could scarcely see through it.

When the doctor arrived with his little bag, he had to pass through my room in order to reach Angelica's. My sisters assembled there with me, and as he went through we hissed him. Presently I peeped through a scratch in the whitewash: my youngest sister was lying almost naked in the middle of her huge bed. I could see her small breasts and tapering shanks quite well; and from one side the doctor was bending over to examine her, while on the other my mother stood guard.

The moment the doctor finally emerged, my half-brother attacked him with a sword. The doctor avoided his thrusts for a few seconds, then pulled out a revolver and aimed. Immediately I dashed between them, striking at the doctor with a tray; the revolver went off and a bullet penetrated the flesh of my right upper-arm. The doctor dressed the wound contemptuously and left.

I did not know what was wrong with Angelica, nor whether she was likely to recover, but I was certain that the doctor's visit had only made her worse. It was growing dusk, and as there seemed nothing I could do to help her, and as I did not feel too ill myself, despite the throbbing of my arm, I decided to go out for a stroll, partly to ease my perturbation, partly to discover something of the countryside in the vicinity and of its so-far-hidden inhabitants.

Not far away from the house, but beyond the cincture of its grounds, stood a dark lake with a forest of giant laurels covering the declivity of its farther verge. A steep and narrow pathway, with steps, had been cut in the trunk of the largest tree, and led up towards its top. As I laboriously mounted this path, I noticed that small houses were perched at intervals where the main boughs branched off. I tried to look into one of these cottages but it was not possible, peer as I would, to see far, because inside each window, a foot or two from the pane, some kind of screen or interior shutter had been drawn across.

The whole scene was now bathed in a greenish radiance having its source in some hidden luminary. Gazing about me, I suddenly perceived that I had

93

wandered into the Green-Light district; that the
woman whom we thought of as 'Mother' was no less
a person than 'Madame', and the doctor's cynical
attentions a formal measure which she was obliged
to take. Small wonder he had barely even considered
our display of hostility; for living as we were, it
would be extraordinary if occasional scenes of dis-
order did not occur, and anyone engaged in his type
of work would soon come to regard them lightly.
They were probably taken as much a matter of
course as a prisoner's impotent batterings on the
door of his cell.

I was puzzled about the presence of Rohan, but
could only assume that perversion was not extinct
amongst my mother's phantom clientèle.

The quiet and the peculiar illumination combined with the appearance of the shuttered houses
to flood a beam of clear if menacing light upon me.
It seemed certain that our mother had made a bar-
gain, if not with the underworld then with the
other world; though what personal profit could
accrue to herself from these transactions it was difficult to guess. Could it be that she sought merely
our humiliation, that to watch our gradual and
painful destruction was for her sufficient reward? If
not, how did the ghosts pay her, and what did they
require in return for their disbursements? Did
they somehow, while feasting an incubus-appetite,

supply its provider with free-passage to hidden
regions?

I fell to speculating anew on the functions of the
young doctor attached to this uncanny establishment. Were his duties purely a matter of form, or
did the lecherous 'revenants' demand freedom from
spiritual syphilis? Or again, was he a cannibal-
surgeon of the mind, a veritable *'mangeur de rêves?'*

I imagine that I indulged in considering these
practical problems simply in order to distract myself from full realisation of our horrible predica-
ment. What future hope could my sisters and I
entertain? Cooped together like pullets, we must
either become lesbian, or resort to the quasi-inces-
tuous touches of Rohan. Unless, indeed, some of us
could bring ourselves to give consent, complete or
partial, to the infernal bargains made on our be-
half, and even grow to enjoy the demonic embraces.

I next tried to guess at the desires of the ghosts
themselves; were they condemned to sterile indul-
gence, or did they think to forge a race of goblins,
vampires, lycanthropes? Had Angelica an intuition
of these terrors so keen that she preferred for herself the prospect of death? Victorina, too, was
puzzled and suspicious, though her more placid
nature forbade her Angelica's extremes; and my
twin-sisters, though at present merely uneasy, might
fall at any moment upon the devastating truth. I

resolved somehow to convince them all of their danger, and then to liberate them from it; though how I was to accomplish this latter project I had no idea. I was handicapped by my scanty knowledge of the phantom lechers' proclivities, though I obscurely felt that I must myself undergo their exigences before I could hope to rescue my sisters. But how at the same time keep my will and senses intact, was the appalling problem with which destiny now faced me.

I descended the tree-path and returned to Troubh. That night my twin-sisters were sleeping in the haunted wing, while Victorina and I shared a smaller room in another part of the house. As soon as we had gone to bed, I laid bare to her all my conclusions; she listened in silence until I had finished.

'I am afraid that what you say is all too true,' she admitted. 'I have guessed at something of the kind from my own experiences, but did not like to think –'

'Listen,' I said, 'it is already too late for hesitation, we must act at once. You must explain the position to the others tomorrow, and I will return to our Uncle's and find some way of rescuing you.'

'What can you do?' wailed Victorina. 'Do stay there quietly; if you meddle with things here, you will only make one more victim.'

'But I am in no better case than you,' I returned.
'I am imprisoned within his demesne,' and I described to her my pitiful attempts at escape. 'If it
were not for my jewels,' I concluded, 'I should
indeed be with you here; but he has some use for
them, evidently, and, strangely enough, some com-
punction about how to obtain them. In this lies the
only hope for any of us.'

'It has always seemed curious to me,' mused
Victorina, 'that you should have inherited the jewels,
though I am the eldest. Do not think, dear, that I
want you not to have them.' she added. 'They are
not the kind of thing I ever wear, and they look
lovely on you. But it is unusual.'

'It is indeed,' I agreed. 'And you have been most
generous about it. But these gems are heavy with
fate, not mere pretty trinkets. Now I must go back,
but be sure that I shall not rest until the mystery
is unravelled, and you are set free.'

I had been dressing myself again during our conversation, and with these words I kissed Victorina
goodbye. My wounded arm scarcely pained me as I
swung myself over the ledge of the open window,
and scrambled to earth by the aid of a tangle of Old
Man's Beard growing up the side of the house. The
night was not dark, and I started out swiftly on the
return journey to my Uncle's.

97

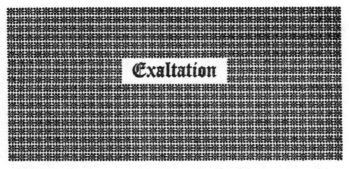

Exaltation

'The myrrh sweet-bleeding in the bitter wound.'
— *Spenser.*

I have remarked earlier upon the visitation which, since living in my Uncle's house, I occasionally experienced. Particularly between sleep and waking would this feeling of attempted possession overtake me; and the very next evening, when I was, I suppose, unusually tired after my adventures at Troubh, I found myself unable to withstand the insidious onslaught.

I can scarcely tell through which sense, if through any, the attack was begun; but I think I first became aware of a faint dizzying perfume that seeped, it may be, through chinks in the wainscot, or under the door. So potent was the scent of this burning drug that I could no longer command my limbs or even raise my head from the pillow; nor could I trust my sight, so dim and contorted did the familiar shapes of my bedroom appear, and this not merely because of the misty wreaths which seemed to form themselves from the air it contained, but because the intoxicating perfume, in filling my nostrils, also disturbed my vision.

Presently it seemed that the door opened without sound and admitted a robed form which might have been that of the Anchorite. This figure glided towards my bed, bent over me and drew back the covers. Hands with scarcely perceptible touch passed along my limbs and torso, making my skin absorb, in the form of an unguent, the same aromatic ingredients the smoke of whose combustion filled the air. Unable to protest, and now even deliciously abandoned to the exciting yet enervating tide, composed of substance so evanescent as to be almost sensation, and feeling so palpable as to be all but substantial, I rapidly swooned.

I must have been borne away beyond the confines of the house, for when I next knew anything I was lying upon some eminence, centre of a grassy open space surrounded with trees, in a remote part of the grounds. The moon was invisible, but it must have been shining, for its pearly light was diffused through a sky of thin cloud. Sound's equivalent to the aromatic odour, a droning music produced from I know not what instruments, arose from the nearby bushes, where a circle of dimly-distinguishable figures crouched in the longer grass. Among these I thought I could at various moments discern my

99

D*

sisters, and then the taller shapes of my Uncle and the Anchorite; in the shadows I seemed to glimpse the inmates of the monastery, and the women I had encountered while making my way towards this island. Later I thought I could see the more sinister or equivocal inhabitants of Troubh – my mother, the doctor, Rohan; and female forms that I took to be dwellers in the tree-houses of the Green-Light district, beckoning to their half-materialised customers. All was shifting; I could not tell whether I saw or fancied I saw these people, even whether I was awake or asleep. Dazed by the phantasmagoria, I turned my eyes away and looked upwards to a still and solid shape towering above me. This was a worn statue, such as often grow in old and neglected gardens, antique in design without, perhaps, being very ancient, a rectangular pillar unhumanised but for a surmounting bearded head of faun or silen, and a tail curling out of the panel furthest away from me. Glancing down at myself, I saw that I was naked except for my jewels.

A wailing sound that sprang from some tubular instrument not hitherto used now entered upon the drone of the music; and I could hear, too, a thudding undertone as of drums, with, rarely, a subdued clash of cymbals. The Anchorite approached me and raised my shoulders, pressing a vessel of some scorching viscous liquid to my lips. Already more

than half-bemused, I had no choice but to drink –
it seemed as though fluid fire were pouring down
my throat and through my veins. The taste was not
merely of burning, but recalled with augmented
intensity the tang of both unguent and fume.

The Anchorite lifted me up – whether or no it
was illusion I cannot tell, but the pull of gravity
appeared to have lost some of its hold over me and
I weighed almost nothing – and set me upon the
image. I embraced the armless torso, finding an
unlooked-for excitement in the pressure of its frigid
moulding. I laid my mouth to its stoney lips, and
a tongue, icy as an adder's, seemed to dart from
between them to meet mine.

I sensed the figure of my Uncle towering behind
me, taller than the statue. Selecting a pliable wand
from a bundle lying beside it, he began to whip me,
while the music increased, clashing more harshly,
drumming more insistently, wailing more stridently.
I could feel a mounting frenzy in the now-invisible
spectators; I could hear their shuffling movements,
sombre breathing and stifled cries as their circle
slowly closed in. Every lash sent a shudder of delight
through me; I saw that my flanks were speckled
with blood, yet I felt no pain from the strokes, only
a stinging unbearable titillation. Clouds of unknown colour and texture were racing past me, wild
corruscations of light, shape and hue; then at a

stroke keener than the rest and a final eruption of music, an icy jet coursed through me to my furthest limbs and I fell insensible.

I awoke next morning as from a profound sleep, but fully clothed. Memories of the night flooding in upon me, I examined myself for some sign that I had been victim of more than delusion. But there was no sign nor symptom; drug, delirium, wounds, rape, all had left me unscathed.

Yet I did not doubt that I had in fact been used by my Uncle for one of his experiments, even though it might have been conducted in the sphere of hallucination. And what had he gained from it? Not my jewels: they rested languidly in their accustomed places, all their stones intact. The thought occurred to me that by my swoon at the climax of the orgy I might unintentionally have thwarted him; that perhaps what he needed was my knowledge of the moment, which, had I possessed it, he could by his subtle arts have filched from me.

Looking about me, I saw that I was not in my own room, but reclining upon a couch in what I now recognised as the ante-room to my Uncle's library.

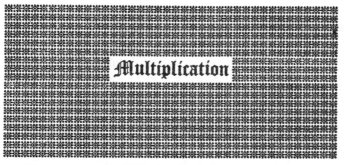

Multiplication

'Between mutability's teeth let us make our
dwelling,
And let her savour us slowly in her contem-
plative way.'

– Rilke.

To the left, an immense archway reared itself; and
shaking off my drowsiness, I got to my feet and
wandered towards it. Above, four painted arche-
typal panels were set into the wall and connected
with a scroll, carved and dimly-gilt, bearing this
legend: 'The All-Wise Doorkeeper, or a Four-fold
Figure, exhibiting analytically to all who enter this
Museum the Mosaico-Hermetic Science of Things
above and Things below.' I entered a long corridor,
from which I could view a series of chambers containing each a sort of emblematic tableau.

Before these began, one was presented with a
panorama of heathery landscape still shrouded in
the misty grey of morning, and featureless but for an
extensive mere. There was little to hold the eye;

yet I could not take my gaze from it; and a remote voice issued as it were from the shining water, softly proclaiming it 'The Silver Morn.' Something made me remember the Anchorite; but if this voice were indeed his, it had become greatly etherealised. The sounds were not repeated, and their spell gradually fading, I passed on to the exhibits proper.

The Book of Lambspring was still in my mind, and remembering its first engraved plate, I recognised that this corresponded with the first chamber; in fact, that the chamber was nothing less than a three-dimensional translation of the engraving. For the entire room, divided from the corridor by a huge pane of glass, formed a tank in which two gigantic fish of the carp family, one incandescent red, the other phosphoric blue, their snouts connected by an all-but-impalpable thread, were swimming languidly round one another in a tireless dance. The water-level reached about two-thirds of the way up the pane, and distant boats sailed across its surface, making voyages to and from the serene landscape that glowed beyond. Suddenly in the sky there appeared, as if inscribed by a lightning-flash, the gnomic words: 'Be warned and understand truly, that two fishes are swimming in our sea.' As I passed on, I saw all fifteen plates ultimately thus given a solid counterpart; and I noticed that many dealt with some aspect of duality.

After this, the compartments changed in character; for it seemed as though my Uncle, hypnotised by the symbolic suits of the Taro, had gathered under their four main categories almost every conceivable object; or rather, that in an attempt to classify specimens of such objects, he had well-nigh lost himself in their diversity. For instance, in the compartment devoted to 'Wands' he had assembled and preserved every imaginable species of leafy branch; and not these only, but also everything that might possibly be called a 'wand', from an axle to a divining-rod; many varieties of walking-sticks also, pencils, brushes, feathers, hair, wings, bones and even portions of furniture, table-legs, carved pilasters, frames.

Under 'Swords' he had collected innumerable objects of metal, weapons of course in great variety, tools and pieces of machinery, though never complete machines – spokes, hat-pins, and indeed anything of a piercing or cutting nature.

In the section for 'Cups' was a most heterogeneous collection of vessels in every kind of material, especially in glass or the more precious metals; but not only these, for almost anything that could hold or contain anything else was here included: cases, boxes, boats in great numbers; flowers, too, of approximately cup-like shape; diagrams and models

of anatomical structures; craters, lake-bed forma-
tions, marine shells.

According to my Uncle's morphological studies,
crazy if you will, though ardently pursued, there
were heaped together under 'Discs' not only everything even roughly disc-shaped, including thousands
of coins in many different materials and of all sizes
and periods; but seemingly everything that he could
lay hands on of a flat and extended form. It was
before this compartment that I paused; not that it
was intrinsically more interesting than its predeces-
sors, for each of them had at first glance given me
the impression of an ill-assorted junk-shop, very
different from the exquisitely-finished tableaux that
brought Lambspring to life; but partly, I suppose,
because I had almost traversed the corridor and was
nearing the final item in the display. For now, my
mind attuned to my Uncle's uncouth approach, I
perceived a relationship between the many examples
of Disc he had collected and the Trump Major
known as the 'Wheel'. There had been several
volumes in the library treating of Taro symbolism,
and from these I had gleaned enough to recognise
certain correspondences. My eyes focussed themselves with special intensity upon a dart-board that
had once been highly-coloured, and I picked it out
of its chaotic heap and began to dust it. Soon I made
out letters spaced at wide intervals round the edge

of its surface – four letters only, spelling the word 'rota'; and though I could hardly explain in words what they conveyed to me, I felt a sensation of ineffable relief. I knew that this simple word held release, both for my sisters and for myself.

The final tableau now presented itself to me; it was the same empty moorland scene as the first, but lacking the mere, and now bathed in the most triumphant sunset glow. The sinking sun was not to be seen, for a gigantic throne rose into the west, superimposing its metallic weight on a good quarter of the sky. The same voice I had heard before, but richer in timbre, extolled 'The Golden Eve'.

I had come to the end of the far-stretching corridor, and, still carrying the board, I opened a door and found myself in the garden. I set the disc bowling like a hoop in the direction of Troubh, and with a sensation of exultant reliance on fate taken at the spin, I let it go. I watched it swiftly gaining momentum down a gentle incline, and knew it would reach its destination. After that, my sisters and half-brother must read its message as I had done, and find in it their freedom.

When I returned to my own apartments, I came upon a rill of pellucid water, not more than ten inches wide, sliding with scarcely a sound over the moss-green carpet of my bed-room. It bubbled up from beneath the wainscot by the window, and flowed diagonally across the floor to disappear under the doorway. I could not find a trace of it in the passage outside, where I suppose it lost itself in the shadows. Making for itself a bed in the pile of the carpet, it seemed no deeper than this, which it filled level with an invisible brink. A few delicate-stemmed flowers like columbines, fritillaries or autumn crocus appeared growing from the carpet near the water, but they looked so fragile that I did not try to pluck them.

I was surprised though not alarmed by this phenomenon, which lasted upwards of half-an-hour and then vanished, leaving the carpet quite dry. I could not explain it, but felt it as a symptom of consolation.

Projection

'*Yo soy la mata inflamada,*
Ardiendo sin ser quemada
Ni con aquel fuego tocada
Que a los otros tocara.'
— *Spanish Song.*

It was not only consolation which was brought me
by the mysterious rill, but something stronger – a
deep conviction that I must get away. I kept to my
room all day, the resolve growing in density and
form. Finally, at a late hour, I opened my door and
peeped into the passage. All was still, and lightless
except for the glass of an uncurtained window at
the end of the landing.

I halted outside the door of my Uncle's study;
there was no sign of an occupant, but I felt certain
that he was there within, waiting. As I have said, I
habitually wore jewellery – several heavy bracelets
and rings, a triple chain forming a collar, a watch,
a big brooch, ear-rings. These I began to tear off; I
flung them all down on my Uncle's threshold, their

109

metallic crash and tinkle echoing through the entranced house. One of the rings rolled away under his door. Then I fled down the passage; and as I turned at the head of the stairway, I caught a last glimpse over my shoulder of the faintly-glimmering heap. The stones gathered within themselves all the light there was in the corridor, and sent it forth again in a muted and reptilian ray.

When I arrived at the massive castellated gatehouse once more, I became aware of the Anchorite's vigilant figure half-hidden at an upper window, but I knew that nothing now could hold me back. I darted towards the square of the archway, but to pass through this, I found that I had to enter the cage of glazed compartments which make up a swing-door; though this was no ordinary swing-door. It contained more than the usual four compartments; and then it was used as a kind of roulette – my sisters were placed one in each section, and all had to run round inside so long as the pivot went on turning.

We were dressed in carnival costume, or ballet-dresses perhaps; and it was my section which remained standing opposite the entrance when the pivot ceased to swing. Rohan was waiting outside.

'You again!' he exclaimed resentfully. 'Why can't I have someone else for a change,' he grumbled casting a longing eye towards one of my twin-sisters,

110

a fluffy-haired brunette, dressed in blue silk, lace
petticoats and pink bows, who was standing on her
points in the compartment next after mine.

I murmured something about fate, intended as an
apology; and Rohan picked me up and slung me
over his back like a goose. I felt as if I were being
held by the neck in a fox's jaws, but I suppose he
did not quite do that.

We started up the road, and soon passed a small
red house with what seemed like a one-storeyed
outhouse built against it. Along the slanting roof
of this a game-bird was suspended face downwards.

'Look at the pheasant!' I cried, by way of divert-
ing him.

And indeed, it was worth looking at. It was very
large, very red and bright; and the scales on its
neck hardly seemed like feathers, they were so huge,
separate and metallic in colour. The tail was long,
with a white plume running down each side to the
tip. I wondered if the bird were quite dead.

Rohan was interested. He turned it over on its
back, stretching it out on a bank of sloping grass.
Then we saw that it was not a pheasant. It was as
big as a woman, and seemed to have a woman's face,
though this was difficult to determine because the
whole head was covered with an opaque membrane
the colour of some ripe citrous fruit. Beneath this
lay the impression of wide cheek-bones, profound

111

sockets and a beak like an eagle's. We could discern
that the beak was open, for its sharpness made the
brilliant yellow membrane almost transparent. The
veil covered the creature's wing-shoulders, and fell
on the breast, which was divided in the centre, like
that of a woman or a bird of prey. I felt that bat-like
hands were folded below; and lower still glowed the
vivid plumage we had seen before, copper-green and
copper-red.

The eagle lay perfectly still, scarcely breathing
and apparently asleep. A voice from the air around
seemed to tell me to leave it undisturbed, and that
one day it would awake from its creative trance.

Immediately I had left the penumbra of my
Uncle's park the air, as yet scarcely touched by
morning, came to my throat with a fresher draught,
and environned me with a more translucid grey. I
ran on now with little sense of direction, borne forward by early breezes that seemed to me the very
breath of liberty, and so buoyant that they might
have been blowing directly off the sea. I had not
shed my clothes with my jewels; yet racing along,
my feet barely touching the moss of the woodland
ride, I had the sensation of being naked and
immersed in some bracing element, as though nothing came between my skin and the soft yet potent
air.

When I regained the main island it was still very

early; and fastening the coracle to the mole from which I had set forth, I made my way to the big deserted house. Ever since my mother had left it, and had ceased to live with my father, I had heard nothing of how he was; and I now began to wonder: How is he managing alone? He never used to be much good at making arrangements for himself. I decided to visit him.

It was only just light when I penetrated the house and mounted to the top-floor; my father had barely finished his bath, and when I called to him he came out immediately into the passage, without dressing, to meet me. This was most unusual for him, as he had never been addicted to nudism.

'How are you?' I cried.

'Very well indeed,' he answered. He seemed delighted to see me and we hugged and kissed. I then suggested as tactfully as I could that he might put on some clothes; and this he did, without apparent embarrassment, as we descended the staircase to the lower floors. He remarked on the amount of jewellery I was wearing; and glancing down suddenly at my gleaming wrists and fingers, I was forced to admit that indeed, for a morning *toilette,* it was perhaps rather much. I saw, too, with astonishment, that what I now wore appeared to be the very trinkets which I had cast from me at my Uncle's threshold.

113

Suddenly the forlorn aspect of the house seemed to strike my father – the carpetless stairs, the uncurtained windows, the bare wood of the floors. He looked about him uneasily as we approached the main hall, and seemed, for the first time since his family's absence, to be taking in his surroundings.

'He does not know he is dead,' I thought. 'Shall I have to tell him?'

But this was not necessary.

'Where are the furnishings?' he asked. 'Why all this emptiness?'

'Don't you realise, father,' I replied gently, pressing his arm with a closer touch, 'that we are no longer living here?'

I paused, then turned for some response; but my father had vanished, utterly melted away, leaving only his old green suit hanging over my arm.

I went into the conservatory-room that led off the rear of the entrance-hall. It was circular with much glass, some white, some tinted with various colours, and was now empty but for the built-in seat running round below the windows. Outside, the encroaching leaves of the garden-shrubs were visible. I waited here for a few minutes perfectly quiet; but my father did not return. Only in the atmosphere of the room there seemed to linger a faint distillation, but whether of sound or colour I could not tell.

I left the conservatory, let myself out of the front
door and made towards one of the side-entrances to
the garden. Here the vegetation had become tropical, recalling that of the antipodes; leaves like open
umbrellas swayed above my head and showers of
warm drops fell through the air. The very light
seemed to have passed through a filter of foliage,
and the exit was clogged with unaccustomed tepid
luxuriance.

There was a low earthy rampart surrounding the
garden and the soil of this had grown volcanic, as
it did from time to time – at least, so I gathered
from some passers-by in the lane outside. Warm
fountains the colour of port-wine were jetting
through the earth, fertilising it to this abundant
growth.

Following the lane, I reached the top of an
incline from which I could see the mountainy
country to the east; and towards this I set my profile. The region was far, but even as I looked its
pencilled summits were touched by the first auroral
glow.